SEE
DICK
RUN

A Grownup's Picture Book

by Joe Randazzo

A Sprezzatura Book
from New Renaissance Press

Sprezzatura Books
New Renaissance Press
8 Woodside Drive
South Burlington, VT 05403

ISBN 978-0-9708279-3-7
Library of Congress Control Number 2009902544

This book is a work of fiction. Character names and incidents in the plot, and depictions in the artwork are products of the author's imagination. Any resemblance to actual events or persons, living or dead, is entirely coincidental.

Front and back covers, photos of interior art,
and author's photograph by Chris Koch.

Artwork on pages 57, 141, and the poem on page 127 are by
Rita Randazzo, used with kind permission.

For Rita:
See Joe Run

Also by Joe Randazzo:

Coffee House
His/Hers: Mars and Venus Write Poetry
  (with Rita Randazzo)
Screen
van Eyck's Secret

PART
ONE

WHITETAIL

See Dick run
with his new kite.

Dick names the kite
Whitetail
because it has
white rag strips tied in knots
hanging from the bottom.

Dick loves the wind in his face
and he hears the paper flapping
as he pulls hard on the string.

He is laughing
louder than the wind.

Whitetail is soaring.

MISTER BUBBLES

There is always time for Mister Bubbles.

Dick likes to stand at the edge of the outfield grass
and launch hundreds of bubbles toward the people
watching Little League baseball.

He will start kindergarten next year.
Dick dreams that someday he'll hit a homerun
over the chain-link fence and into the parking lot.

He is using the small wand end, the one that makes
many tiny bubbles. He pretends they are space aliens
who will destroy anyone who touches them.

Dick, Sam, and Tasha often go to Southside Park
with Sam's mother. She is very nice and takes them
almost every weekend.

Tasha tells Dick she has no more Mister Bubbles.
Sometimes Sam's sister can be a real pain.
Dick doesn't like girls very much, but he pours half
his bottle into Tasha's empty one.

He remembers a Saturday afternoon last January
when he and Tasha went to the park. It was so cold,
the bubbles they blew froze and bounced on the
ice skating rink! All the children tried to catch them.

Dick likes to do fun things that make people happy.

DICK'S ROOM

Dick is being punished.

He isn't allowed to go outside this Saturday morning
because he didn't do his homework last Tuesday.

Dick is sitting in his room, upstairs in the back dormer.
He is looking out the window at Sam and Tasha's house,
the big white one on the hill.

His friends often wave to him from the meadow,
where they run and play with their dog, Barney.
Dick's father won't let him have a dog of his own,
because they are dirty and bark too much.

Dick's room was very messy this morning, with toys
and clothes scattered all over the floor, so he got
punished again. His mother yelled at him and slapped him.

She did bring him some animal crackers later,
when he had picked his things up, but he didn't want
them and threw them out the window.
Then he wished he had them.

Dick's mother smelled funny this morning,
just like last weekend when her friends came over
for a party. There was a lot of shouting and loud music.

Dick wonders how come he gets yelled at
every time his mother smells like cough medicine.

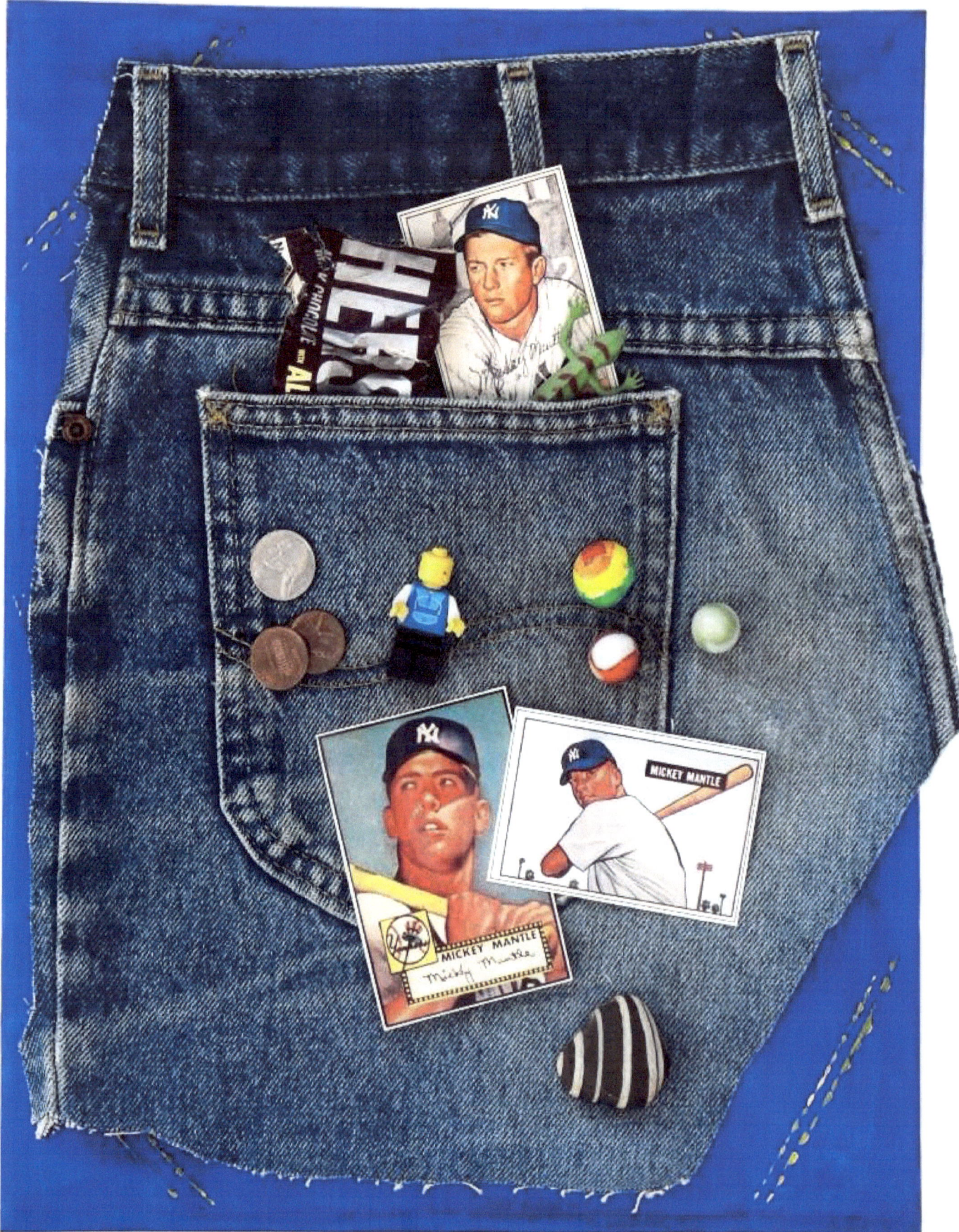

ROBOT MAN

Dick carries his Mickey Mantle baseball cards
wherever he goes.
Someday he is going to be just like Mickey.
Mickey doesn't have to do any homework.

Today, along with Robot Man and Green Lizard,
he also carried home his first-grade report card.
It has a D for attentiveness. His teacher wrote
a note at the bottom that said he needed to
concentrate more and stop fidgeting.
She also said that he talks too much in class.

He hates his teacher, hates school, and
sometimes he even hates his parents.

He hates the ugly brown rusty bars around
each classroom window,
hates the red and white school tie he has to wear,
and the hash with mashed potatoes they serve for lunch,
hates the big textbooks which are too heavy to carry,
and the driver of the yellow bus who keeps telling
him to stop singing so loudly and sit in his seat.

When things aren't going very well,
Dick brings his favorite small toys with him.
He feels comforted knowing they are there,
and plays with them when no one is looking.
Lately both his front pockets have been full of toys.

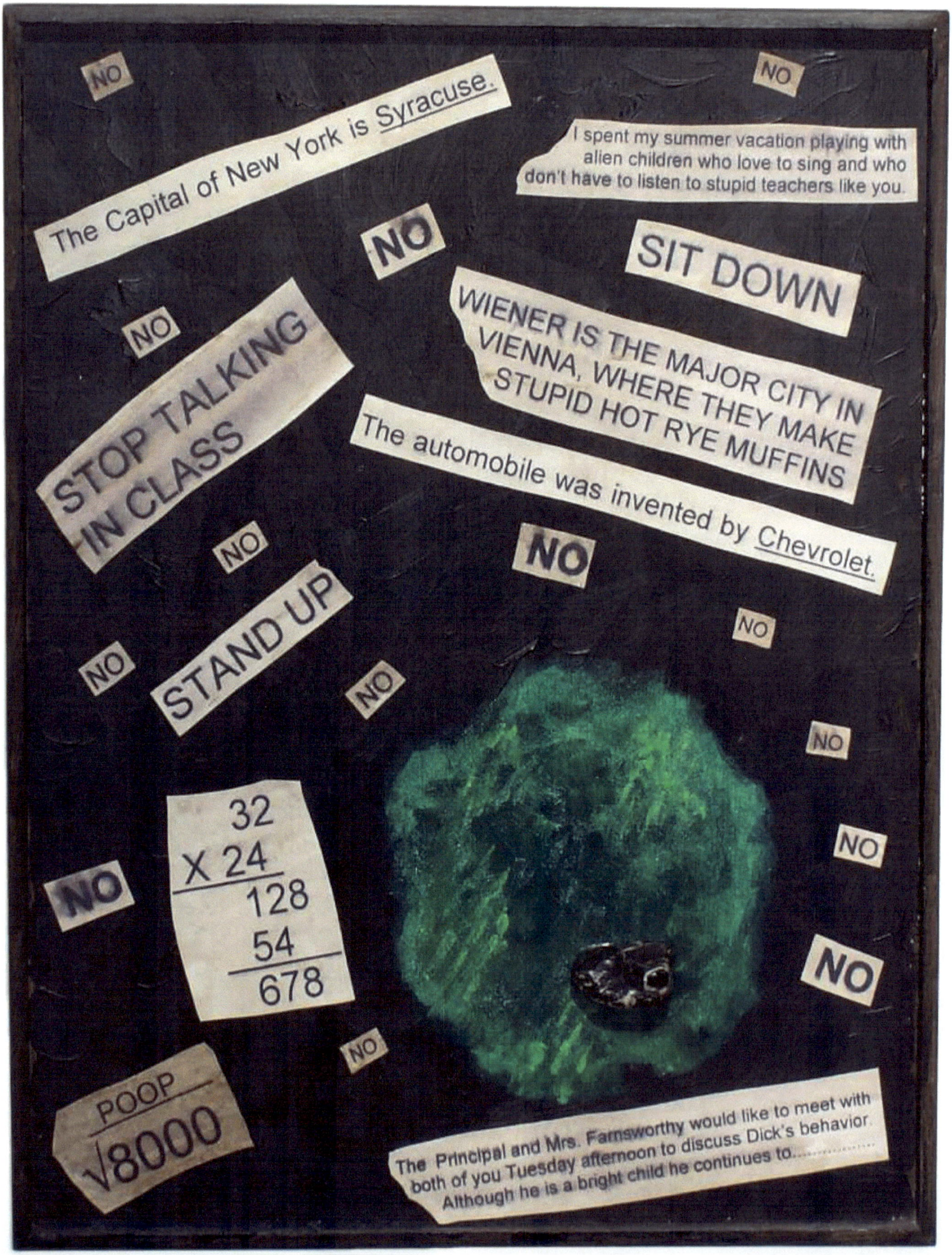

NO

NO

The Capital of New York is <u>Syracuse.</u>

I spent my summer vacation playing with alien children who love to sing and who don't have to listen to stupid teachers like you.

NO

NO

SIT DOWN

STOP TALKING IN CLASS

WIENER IS THE MAJOR CITY IN VIENNA, WHERE THEY MAKE STUPID HOT RYE MUFFINS

The automobile was invented by <u>Chevrolet.</u>

NO

NO

NO

STAND UP

NO

NO

NO

NO

NO

$$\begin{array}{r} 32 \\ \times\ 24 \\ \hline 128 \\ 54 \\ \hline 678 \end{array}$$

NO

NO

$$\sqrt[POOP]{8000}$$

NO

The Principal and Mrs. Farnsworthy would like to meet with both of you Tuesday afternoon to discuss Dick's behavior. Although he is a bright child he continues to.....

WILLOW ROCK

Whenever Dick is troubled, he visits Southside Park and
sits on a large boulder hidden by hemlock trees
and draped by a huge willow.

The top has been worn smooth by all the people climbing
on it. He sneaks out of school by the east entrance when
everyone goes to lunch, and he races half a mile to his
favorite place. If anyone else is on the rock he is disappointed
and sits somewhere on the grass.

Today he is alone with his peanut butter and jelly sandwich,
four Oreo cookies, and a can of warm Hires Root Beer.

He pokes at the silver flecks on top of the rock with a two-blade
pocket knife and removes a small piece of mica.

He does not want to go back to school and study
the square root of 8000.

He must be evil.
He doesn't mean to do wrong things. He doesn't
think they are wrong, so he doesn't tell Father Doyle
at confession.

He wonders if he will go to Hell.

THIRD PLACE

The District Science Fair had sixty-seven
projects from five elementary schools.
There were robots and chemistry demonstrations,
homemade calculators, and cameras.
Dick's exhibit used special rotating sunlamps
and prisms to reflect a face-like image
on a vertically placed white board.

He races home with the news.
"I won a prize at the Science Fair!
I won a prize at the Science Fair!"

"That's nice, dear,"
his mother replies.
"What did you build, an electric car?"

"What kind of prize,"
his father asks.
"What kind of prize did you win?"

I won this ribbon.

"That's for third place.
Why couldn't you have won first place?
Those other kids
aren't better than you are."

ZACH'S BAY

Dick and his father drove for five hours.
It was the happiest day he could remember,
all the way to Zach's Bay to the very end of Fisherman's Pier.

It was the first time Dick had seen saltwater.
The smell of the brine, of the squid they were using for bait, and of
the gas and oil smoke in the outboard motors was incredible.

If only Sam and Tasha could see him now. His father shows him how
to put squid on the three hooks attached to a triangular-shaped, four-
ounce lead sinker, with a silver spoon swiveling about two feet in
front of the weight.

"What's that shiny thing for, Dad?"
"Attracts the fish to the bait, then they bite the hook and we got dinner."

They both let out line. Three seagulls land on the railing near them,
wanting a handout, and Dick hears their caw-cawing for the first time.
Wow, they are so close he can almost touch them. How white they are
in the sunlight. After a while, he reels in his line to check the bait. The
reel makes a ticking sound like his bicycle. Another fisherman pulls up
a square trap with a crab that looks like a giant spider. The tip of his
father's pole bends down sharply and he brings up a strange-looking
fish that puffs up like a softball.

"That's a blowfish, son, and he's trying to frighten us by making himself
bigger, so we'd better throw him back."
For an instant, the fish floats on the surface of the water, then darts
beneath the surface like a deflated balloon.

Dick feels a big tug on his line a reels in a flat fish with a white bottom,
a black top, and both eyes on one side of its head.
"What's that?"
"That's dinner, m'boy, that's dinner.
It was the happiest day he could remember.

14

A DAY AT THE BEACH

Dick's Aunt Grace always calls him Richard. She calls his father
Thomas, even though everyone else calls him Tom.

Last night they slept over at her house, and today they are going
to Jones Beach. Dick's father and Aunt Grace sit on a blanket
under a big yellow and green umbrella, talking.

They tell Dick he may walk down the beach away from the swimming
area, but not to wander too far. Dick picks up shells and smooth
stones as he walks along the waterline, and stuffs his pockets full.
A little kid is filling Dixie cups with wet sand, working on a neat fort.
The kid's father is fishing with a long surf rod and has caught a big
fish. The kid opens up the cooler. Dick asks what kind of fish it is.
A striped bass, the man answers. Dick stays awhile helping to
build the fort, then continues on his walk.

He is suddenly overwhelmed with joy. Everything is so new!

Sandpipers scurry back and forth, just ahead of the incoming foam.
The blue-green water tumbles higher and higher as the tide comes in.
He likes the small of suntan lotion, and the rubbery feel of kelp
washed ashore. Sand dollars, horseshoe crabs, and razor-clam shells
roll in and out with the surf. Dick stares at huge fishing trawlers and
girls in bikinis, the biggest horizon and the smallest swimsuits
he has ever seen.

Dick looks outbound into a landless seam where the sky curves down
to meet the ocean, and says a prayer that he will return to this place.

He picks up a solitary scallop shell, and replaces it with his pocket
knife. Dick thinks of it as offering a piece of himself, a trade of blood
brothers' treasure.

Now the sea will always be within him.

National Rifle Association
OFFICIAL 50 FT. SLOW FIRE PISTOL TARGET

1-31
2-46

MATCH # _____

RELAY # _____

TARGET # _____

STAGE # _____

4   5   6   7   8   9   10

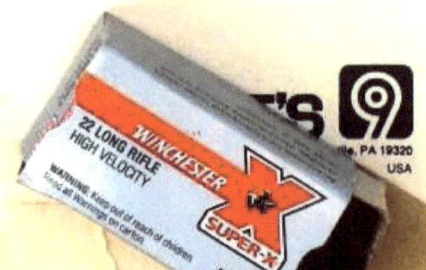

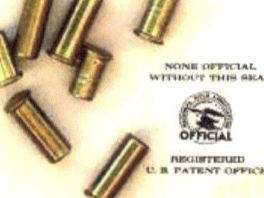

NONE OFFICIAL
WITHOUT THIS SEAL

OFFICIAL

REGISTERED
U. S. PATENT OFFICE

NRA #B2

STEADY PRESSURE

"Okay, now listen carefully. You line the front sight in the notch of the rear sight and put the black part of the target right on top of it like it was a lollipop."

"Dad, do I have to?"

"Yes, all men should learn how to shoot. I'll go first. Remember to always stand behind the shooter. You pull the hammer back, take a deep breath, and exhale as you put steady pressure on the trigger. Don't jerk it or you'll pull your shot off. We'll each shoot five shots."

Dick puts both hands over his ears as his father empties a cylinder down range. They both check the target.

"31, not bad. Now I'm loading in some shorts. They don't have any kick and make less noise."

Tomorrow, July 17th, is Dick's eleventh birthday. As a present, his parents took him camping in the Catskill Mountains, where his father hunts deer every November. Tonight will be his first night sleeping in the wild.

"Aw Dad, do I have to?"

Dick holds the single-action six-gun with both hands and does as instructed. He shoots quickly because the gun is heavy and difficult to hold.

"That's too fast! Too fast! You probably jerked your shots."

"Can we do something else, Dad?"

"Dick, let's go look at the target. 46? 46?
Holy shit! Evelyn look at this, he shot a 46.
The kid's a natural."

CAMPOUT

The Brown family has a neat pop-up camper that folds out in two directions, but Dick's mom and dad let him sleep in his official Boy Scout pup tent about one hundred feet away from their site.

"Don't forget now, honey, if you get scared you just come back inside," his mom reassures him.

At ten o'clock the campfire starts to die down and Mr. Brown shuts off the double-mantle gas lantern. Dick crawls into his tent, turns on his flashlight and begins reading a Superman comic book.

After a while the used batteries turn the light yellow and he yawns, tired out from the day's excitement.

He hears his parents laughing and is glad that, for now, they aren't fighting. For half an hour there is complete stillness, not even leaves rustling in the wind, nothing. He snuggles inside his sleeping bag and zips it shut.

Almost asleep, he hears something scurrying on the pine needles next to his tent. Maybe it's a bobcat or a coyote! His flashlight shines just brightly enough for him to glimpse a field mouse about ten feet away. He thought it must have been something much bigger. Then there is a loud screeching sound, cree, cree, cree, cree, in the trees right over the tent. Is that an owl or a hawk? Maybe he should go sleep in the camper.

He decides to stay put, and listens to the crickets. He enters that middle land between awake and dreaming and pretends he is an explorer on safari. Suddenly he hears the sound of twigs breaking and fast, deep breathing. He slowly opens the mosquito netting and shines his light into the forest.

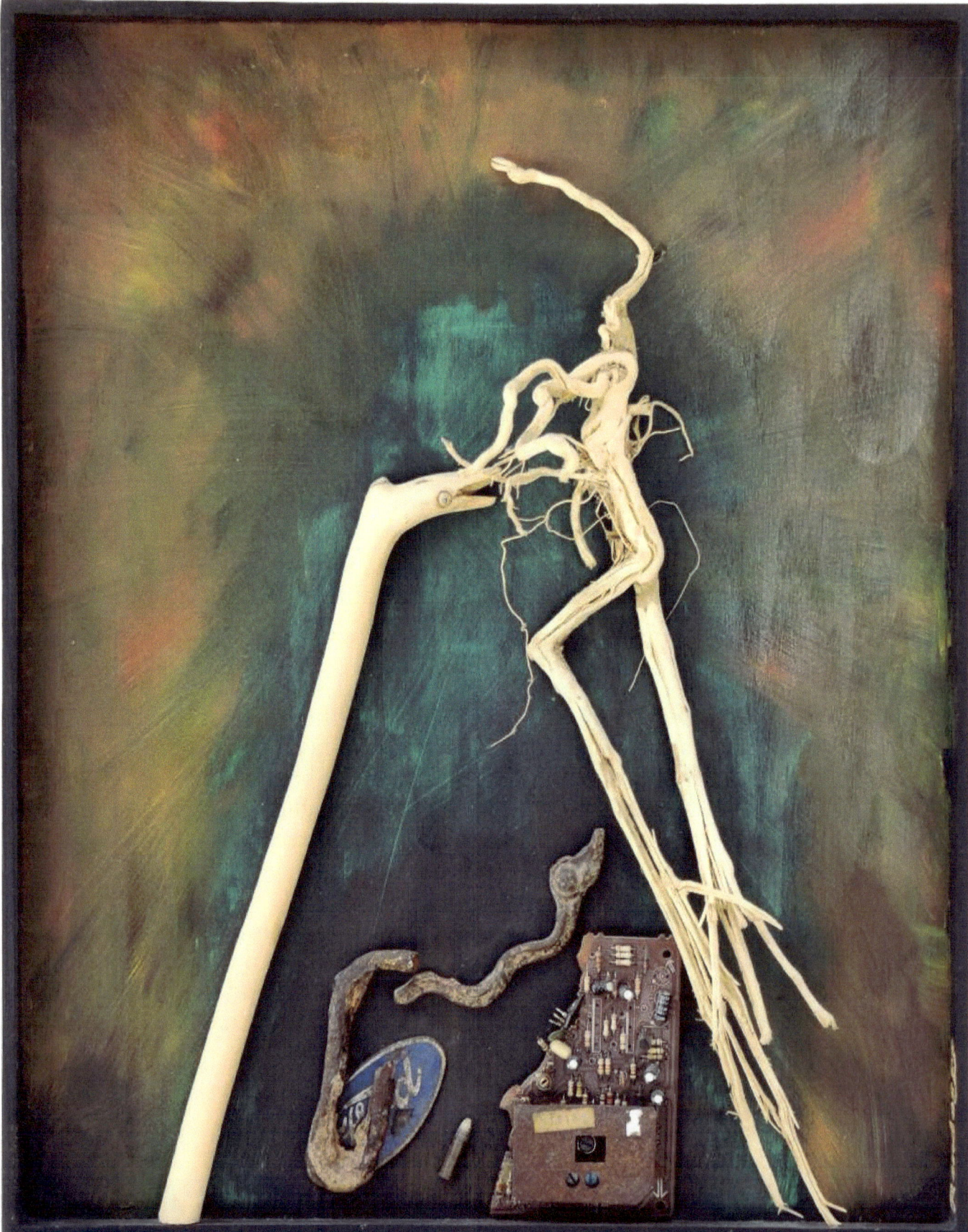

MONSTERS

Alongside the Whitehorse River,
half a mile from his campsite,
Dick finds something really neat.

An old stone foundation, charred wood, and debris are all that
remain of a cabin homestead hidden deep in the woods.
It is almost completely overgrown with white birch trees
and raspberry bushes. Now only red boomer squirrels and
black-capped chickadees live there.

Dick picks up a Model T Ford emblem and stuffs it and other
rusty parts into his pockets. Father along the river he finds two
pieces of driftwood and carries everything home.

At night in bed, on his green comforter, he arranges the objects
he found and holds a piece of driftwood in each hand.

The two monsters fight over an ancient civilization.
They bite each other in the neck and blast each other's arms
and legs off as they battle over the treasure.

I'll kill you, you goddamned jerk.
Bam! Bam! Pow! Slam!
You're gonna die, retard.
Bam! Bam! Pow! Slam!
Die, jerk, die.

BOY SCOUT

"Dad, when can we go back to the beach?"

"I don't know," his father answers.
"Maybe sometime next summer."

"Then can I go to Southside pool with Sam and Tasha?"

Tasha is changing. She is filling out on top and getting
curvy. The other girls in his class are also changing.
They suddenly seem older than the boys. Dick likes
to watch them move, likes the way their
school uniforms cling.

He likes the way he feels when he is alone
with his thoughts of them
and of the girls he saw lying on the sand
at Jones Beach.

If this is what growing up is all about,
he wants to grow up fast.

"Dad, I don't think I want to stay in the Boy Scouts
after all. Could I join the 4H Club instead?
Sam and Tasha are in 4H."

"4H? What for? You want to raise sheep? 4H is
for cattle farmers and petunia growers. The Boy
Scouts are for young men who want to be leaders."

"Don't you want to be a leader?"

SEED

"What are you doing in there?" Father Doyle yells.
"You better not be playing with yourself!
That stuff is seed, you save it or when you're married.
Otherwise it's a mortal sin and you'll go
straight to Hell."

Frightened, Dick replies that he is only
reading a comic book.
"Let me see it then," Father Doyle orders.
Dick slides the comic under the wooden door
of the stall.

"Archie? This is what you read?
Absolute garbage, go back to your classroom."

Dick's last year at St. Boniface is spent dodging
the monsignor, the priests, Sister Mary Ellen,
his parents, and two goody-goody classmates
who always rat on him.

Dick steals one of his uncle's Playboy magazines.
He and Sam spend Thursday's lunch hour on
Willow Rock checking it out. They giggle
excitedly, stroking the girls in the pictures,

until Father Doyle sneaks up on them.

DICK'S HAMMER

There is a repetitive pounding sound of metal on metal
and shattering glass coming from behind the school.

Dick is using a large ball-peen hammer and is getting tired
from all the work. First he does the front and then the left
side, followed by the right side, finishing to the rear.

He does a good job making indentations on all surfaces.

Officer Perez approaches the driveway and meets Father
Doyle, who is gesturing wildly. They head for the parking lot.

Dick doesn't know or care who the old car belongs to, he just
smashes the shit out of it. When he sees the lights of the
police cruiser he jumps over the fence.

They don't spot him, and he hides behind a green dumpster
until the patrol car is out of sight.

He runs home and calmly says hello to his parents. Dick pulls
the hammer out from under his jacket and returns it to his
father's toolbox.

His mother looks up hazily from her fourth double.
"How was Boy Scouts, dear?"

"Fine."

Tasha, the girls from Southside pool, the girls he saw at
Jones Beach and in Playboy, Sister Mary Ellen and his mother,
all race in a blur across his dreams.

Dick cries himself to sleep.

FIRST DAY LOCKOUT

Numbers 435 and 437
are being used by two eleventh graders.
They won't let Dick near his locker,
number 436.

He is sandwiched between them.
They leave their doors open to block his path,
and they both are a foot taller than he is.

Dick calmly waits for them to leave.
He turns the dial 32, 45, 17, but it remains locked.
Maybe it was 45, 32, 17? Nope.
How about 35, 42, 17? Still won't open.

He has forgotten the combination.
The piece of paper that has the numbers
is on the small table next to his bed.
No one is home, and he decides against
going to the main office.

He carries his jacket, lunch, and gym clothes
to first period study hall.
The bell has already rung
and all the other seventh graders are seated
when he enters the room.

As he turns to shut the door,
Dick's lunch bag rips open
and a thermos of chocolate milk
shatters when it hits the floor.

MR. K

"Okay girls, everyone takes two laps around the track, everyone takes a shower, and everyone cleans out his locker. If I see any crap on the floor, tomorrow I'll run you till you drop. Is that clear? Are you listening, Noodlebrain?"

> *What an asshole. Who do you think you are,*
> *a Marine drill instructor?*

"You've got to grab the rope with both your feet, Peabrain, or you won't make it to the top."

> *Bite it, motormouth.*

"Why didn't you go to the bathroom before you came outside, Sissybrain?"

> *Because I wanted to piss on you, Mr. Korevski.*

"You have to jump higher, Donkeybrain, the basket isn't going to come down to you."

> *Jump off a bridge, you psychopath.*

"Pigeonbrain, carry the equipment bag."

> *Korevski, crawl into a body bag and die.*

"Pigeonbrain, did I just hear you say something?"

> "No sir," *you fart blossom.*

IT AIN'T ME BABE

The Key Club, the Glee Club, the Chess Club,
Young Americans for Freedom,
the lacrosse team, and the Thespians.

If you can't act in a major or even a bit part, we can
still use you around here to paint backdrops or help
the players with their makeup and costumes.

Go Spartans go, fight team fight,
I want everyone to shout a little louder,
this is a pep rally, not the library.
Let me hear you scream.
Go Spartans go, fight team fight,
where's your school spirit?

Oooooo, gross. Someone spit in your
mashed potatoes and you ate it.
Yuk, didn't you see it?

Hey Bo Bo, check out the fink;
expensive clothes, expensive shoes,
my, my, don't he look special.

Hey, Mike's got green glass beads, groovy.
Sylvia's had a nose job,
Sylvia's had a nose job.
John's got leather sandals
and he scored some acid.
Wow, man, that's cool.

Hey Dick, where're you going?

Dr. Timothy Leary

J.D. Salinger

BBC

THE SPARTAN NON-CONFORMIST

Jean Paul Sartre

Jack Kerouac

BBC

Janis Joplin

Bob Dylan

Albert Camus

THE SPARTAN NON-CONFORMIST

THE SPARTAN NON-CONFORMIST

Allen Ginsberg

THE SPARTAN NON-CONFORMIST

Dick shows Tasha a copy of Volume I, No. 1
of his new underground newspaper.

"Wow! Cool! How did you print it?"
She looks at the stack of freshly stapled sheets.

"There's a letterpress department at my father's office. He said they
would do it if I bought the paper." Dick proudly reads selected
paragraphs from his editorial, "Rising Above the Level of Mediocrity."
He quotes Marx and Sartre on the middle class and adds his own
"...we don't need three televisions and two big cars. Don't let them
brainwash you into reliving your parents' tired dreams.

"There's an article about the football team getting drunk after
Saturday's game. They shoved and taunted Jeremy because he dropped
a pass in the end zone that would have won the game. Coach Korevski
saw them and did nothing to stop it."

Tasha asks Dick if he put his name on it. He just grins and says that
the newspaper is written by the Phantom. "I'm just going to sneak
copies in and leave them everywhere." She reads the feature article on
page one. "Oh, my God! Mr. Carmino got DWI'd in New Jersey, and
he's been picked up for assaulting his mother-in-law. He's my
health-class teacher."

"Guess who was seen sitting on the principal's lap? Right here on page 2."

"No! You gotta be kidding."

"Right here on page 2. This ought to shake things up a bit."

Tasha looks shyly up at Dick through her long eyelashes and in a
quiet voice asks him if she can help with the newspaper.

"Sure, let's work tonight."

VOLUME I, No 2   EDITORIAL

AN OPEN LETTER TO THE U.S. ARMY
RECRUITER WHO WAS HERE LAST WEEK.

DEAR SERGEANT DAVIS:
WAR IS GOOD BUSINESS, INVEST YOUR SON.

BUT THAT'S ME YOU'RE TALKING TO.
I'M HOLDING THE GIRL I LOVE AND I'M
NOT GOING TO VIETNAM.

NAPALM, THE VIETCONG, B17, B29, B52,
BINGO! YOU WIN AN ALL EXPENSE PAID
TRIP TO THE SCENIC MEKONG DELTA. YOU GO,
OR SEND YOUR OWN KID, BUT LEAVE US ALONE.

DID YOU EVER HEAR...

...a Martin twelve-string guitar with new strings on it?
Sounds better than an incoming mortar round. Sounds
a whole lot better than your empty promises and lies.

Does that M16 feel good in your hands?

Tasha feels good in mine.

You say we have to kill for survival, kill to preserve
democracy, kill for peace, kill to influence others, kill
to impress, or is it kill just for the hell of it?

Your penis doesn't work properly, so you shoot that big 45.
Do you have a woman who loves you or do you get a hardon
when you see a cluster bomb?

If you love another human being and are loved in return,
how can you kill someone who you don't even know
and who is also loved by their family?

Hell no, we won't go!

Stop the war, stop it now!
Stop the war, stop it now!
Stop the war, stop it now!

OH, YOU BEAUTIFUL DOLL

Tasha will be seventeen on Sunday.
Dick goes shopping for a gift at the Lions Club flea market.

He calls Tasha "Dollface," and she likes to wear big hats, so when
he finds the sheet music he flips out. Tasha has straight auburn
hair and is 5 feet 11 ½ inches tall, about an inch taller than Dick.
He is one year older and will graduate from high school in June.

It will make a cool present. He also finds a black-velvet painting
of Elvis and brings it home, too. He strips off the backing and
removes the velvet Elvis. He dreams of removing Tasha's clothes.

He cuts an oval piece of poster board and paints it blue.
He remembers three weeks ago when she said I love you.
He cannot think of anything else.

Dick's mother gives him some lace curtain fabric which he
stretches over the poster board. His soul stretches to the open
road and to the two of them driving, driving west to no place in
particular. If only they had a car.

He glues the sheet music in place and closes the frame back.
He hears her voice in his daydream.

He ties braided picture wire to two eyelets.
He watches her move in his daydream.

He wraps the present in blue and gold colored paper.
They make love and run away in his daydream.

He crisscrosses red ribbon on the package and ties a large bow.
Happy birthday, Dollface.

FIRST LOVE

There will never be another first time.
Skin against my skin.

There will never be another.
How ripe against my chest.

There will never be another first time.
She has opened.
He has risen.

MEXICO

Dick has just heard the news.
Evelyn Brown was quite drunk
and crying uncontrollably, but he could still
understand what his mother was saying.

Thomas Brown has left the country.
His father's note was short, simple, and to the point.

"I have gone from our household for good. For me this is
the only way. I divided all our assets into house, money,
and possessions. I took way less than half my share but did
take most of our savings. You keep the house and what's in
it. You still have $10,000, that should buy you enough time
to dry out and find a job. Dick is old enough to look after
himself. I am sailing from somewhere on the Yucatan
Penninsula, so don't bother trying to locate me."

Without speaking, Dick races upstairs and throws everything,
everything that was Thomas Brown into cardboard cartons.
He empties the model 1911 Colt 45 automatic from his father's
closet and sticks it in his belt. He takes all the other stuff to
the landfill.

He drives to Willow Pond and throws the gun at least
twenty-five yards, into the middle of the
cool, deep, still water.

BLOWIN' IN THE WIND

Dr. Codger, Principal, Southside High School:
"So you are the person responsible for printing this trash! I knew I'd catch you sooner or later. Brown, you are out of here for a week. That will teach you to report on my personal life, you little bastard. No college will take you now. There are no scholarships for suspended, under-achieving radicals. There goes your S2 rating. Tenhut!"

Evelyn Brown, mother:
"I'd love to give you tuition money, hon, but we've got to have something to live on. I just can't sell the house. Could you get a job and go to school nights? I'll get a job as soon as I can, I promise."

Tasha Beekman, friend and only love:
"But I'm not ready to get married! We're both too young. Let's wait until we finish college. I got that basketball scholarship at Hofstra."

Sam Beekman, best friend:
"I've had my fill of this place. It's time for a little adventure, so I've decided to join the Navy and become a pilot. They give you good training, and I can fly commercial jets when I get out. You've got no money for school, you ought to think about joining up. You don't have to bomb Vietnam, you can fly transport choppers."

Timothy Potts, Personnel Director, Charles Ponzi Banking & Insurance:
"Mr. Brown, we learned that you just graduated from school and have a high draft-lottery number. The war will be over soon, anyway we are not worried about it at Charles Ponzi, no siree bob. We have an entry-level Underwriter's position available for you. It won't make you rich but with a little hard work..."

Clyde Burgess, drummer for Argamemnon:
"What's happening, Sir Richard? Hey, those guitar licks of yours are pretty cool. Our rhythm player just split. We got lots of work, chicks, acid, good stuff. You know of a better life? Whatdayasay?"

PART TWO

ARGAMEMNON

Fake, fake, fake,
You ask me if I care,
Will I always be there,
But you just fake, fake, fake.

> The grille of the bass amplifier
> smells like burnt grass and
> spilled beer and it rattles like hell
> on low E.

Fake, fake, fake,
This is more than I can take,
There must be some mistake,
All you do is fake, fake, fake.

> "Clyde, you're draggin', man.
> If you can't handle that shit
> don't do it. This is an important
> gig and we want to sound good."

Fake, fake, fake,
You're always on the make,
All you do is take,
You just fake, fake, fake.

> "Bring the gain up on rhythm guitar.
> Okay, harmony on the last chorus.
> That's it, we're cookin' now,
> we're cookin'."

THE FIRE DOWN BELOW

Back beat, down beat, I feel my heart beat,
or is it the floor tomtom and the conga
pulse of two a.m. across smoky tables,
and me looking at you diggin' me and my music.

Someday, outside, somewhere in the Los Angeles
Coliseum, Yankee Stadium, or in some
mega-meadow, I will have a wall of sound
fifty feet high and an ocean of chicks
screaming for more Me, more Me.

When the sun goes down I will be the
hydrogen flare that bathes the night
airwaves with music and my words of
happiness and my words cutting down
the world's sorry asses shall reverberate.
I will not be turned off.

The PA system of my soul will be set
at ten and you will hear me.
I will not be turned off.

Someday.
Somewhere.
Somehow.
I will be Somebody.

NIGHTHAWK

"Hey Dick, I got chain oil
all over my new jacket."

"Sorry Debbie, this is a Nighthawk,
not your father's Oldsmobile."

I like to feel the wind in my hair,
I like 0-60 in 5 seconds.
No one on the road is faster,
no one on the road is better.

"Dick, you play a mean guitar.
This is good shit, is it Panama red?
Can I buy a nickel bag?
You got a roach clip?
Dick, can I stay here tonight?"

"It makes no difference to me."

"Do you want to make love?"

"I've got nothing better to do.

"Yes, this is good shit.
Debbie, you better walk home,
or I'll call a cab."

Alone I can hit 130 miles per hour
on my Nighthawk.
No one on the road is faster,
no one on the road is better.

FATHER DOYLE

"Father Doyle! What are you doing in here?"

"I heard you were in a band, so I stopped by to say
hello. You sound pretty good, but you know, I was
raised on Tommy Dorsey and Rosemary Clooney.
Who's that girl I saw on your motorcycle?"

"Which one, the blonde? Her name is Debbie."

"What happened between you and Tasha? You seemed
so good together."

"She's got more important things to do... I don't want to talk about it."

"Did you ever hear from your father?"

"He can go straight to hell."

"How's your mom doing?"

"We don't speak much. Excuse me, I've got to do the last set."

"Richard, I know you had a rough time in school, and I made
some mistakes I really regret, but..."

"Who cares? That's ancient history."

"I wasn't quite ready for a new car, you know. I saw you hiding
behind that dumpster. You had such a rage inside you, I didn't
know what to do."

"Sorry about the car. I didn't know it was yours. Just forget about it."

"For God's sake, son, don't smoke marijuana and shoot the heroin.
That stuff will kill you."

"Just leave me alone, Father."

ROCK & ROLL

At 3:00 a.m. in late November
Southside Park is deserted.
Willow Rock is wet
and slippery from freezing drizzle.

The solitary street lamp,
a halo in the mist at the edge of the ballfield,
provides just enough light
for Dick to prepare his potion
of white powder into liquid.

He injects it deep into his being and
hears a hissing sound inside his head.
For an instant
the surface of his soul cools a little,
but underneath the hot lava keeps flowing.

Dick loses consciousness
and slides down Willow Rock.

ST. VALENTINE'S DAY MASSACRE

"You're the only person
I've ever been with.
Don't I mean anything to you?
I really loved you.

"Look at you!
You look terrible.
What are you supposed to be,
a rock star?

"You had such a beautiful soul.
You were a writer, not a druggie.
Now you're just another second-rate
guitar player who's screwed
up in the head."

"You wouldn't go away with me, remember, Tasha?
You'd rather be a second-rate basketball player.
Just leave me alone."

"Grow up, grow up!
Don't try and lay a guilt trip on me,
you son of a bitch.
Don't you know how much I care for you?"

"Leave me alone, Tasha.
Go back to school."

SEE DICK RUN AWAY

Dick packs what he can carry
and says goodbye to no one.
He boards the Greyhound bus
and arrives in New York City at 11:45 p.m.
with two hundred thirty-seven dollars
in his wallet.

The subway station stinks of urine.
The YMCA room is small
and vibrates with each passing train.

There is shouting and the sound of
broken glass on the street below.
He is feverish from a bad cold and
hasn't eaten since he threw up his lunch.

Dick has only one thought,
one plan,
one reality.

He is going to try and sleep
on that metal-framed cot
and wake up the next morning,
hopefully in a different world.

Dick's body hurts so bad
from no drugs,
he feels so sick,
maybe he won't wake at all.

ALONE

Dick has a job and a small apartment
on the Lower East Side.

At first he smokes pot once in a while,
but lately there's been no money left
after paying for rent and food.

Fourteen stories above tar and asphalt,
he is on steel stilts, surrounded by concrete
so predators can't get at him.

He does not know any of his neighbors,
and hides in his anonymity.
He refuses to have any expectations,
and suppresses his desire to
create words, to play music, or to be
close to another human.

Dick reads.
He comes home after work and reads.

For fourteen straight months: Whitman, Garcia Lorca,
George Santayana, Allen Ginsberg, William F. Buckley, Jr.

He reads.

William Carlos Williams, e e cummings, Dante,
William Faulkner, Socrates, Dylan Thomas.

Cockroaches crisscross the bathroom and kitchen floors.
He has no telephone, no television.

He reads.

DEAD END

The chalk outline and bloodstains were shocking.
Yellow tape reading "Do Not Cross Police Line"
again blocked the north entrance to his building.

The second murder on his street in five weeks drives
Dick out of Manhattan. He finds a decent
apartment in Jackson Heights and gets
a job working in the neighborhood camera shop.

The people before him had lived in the apartment
for twenty years, so thanks to rent control, the landlords
could only raise the rent fifteen percent.
He pays $95 a month, less than one-sixth of
the rent on the East Side.

He is across the street from a small park and watches
the children playing. The smell of Indian food is everywhere.

For the first time since he fled to New York City
Dick reaches out to someone.
An old woman has tripped and fallen on the street.
Dick helps her up and carries her groceries back to her
apartment, the lady leaning on him for support.

This simple kindness ends Dick's isolation.
The door has been opened.
Now his thoughts are of home, his
mother's drinking, his father's running away,
Sam, Tasha, Argamemnon, Father Doyle.

Someone, something, anything other than himself.
His self has turned into a dead end.

PRODIGAL SON

"I knew you would come home when you were ready. I did a lot of praying."

Evelyn Brown has been sober for almost two and a half years.
She is teaching high school again and has redecorated the house.

"Except for your room, Dick. That's as you left it. I keep the door open a couple of inches like you used to do before you went to sleep at night."

They hug and talk, and then talk some more. The lost weeks and months become sentences, and milestones unfold as chapters, tenderly spoken to each other.

"Your father is in Greece. He keeps sending me letters. He wants to come home. At first I told him to forget it, but I really do miss him. Things would be different now. I can't be a victim anymore."

Dick becomes angry and reminds her of how they were abandoned.

"We all make mistakes, hon, and sometimes we change for the better. I'm sorry I wasn't there for you, but I am here for you now. Look at you and Tasha. Look at your own life. You trashed that girl, you trashed yourself, but you survived. You've grown. Should I turn *you* away?"

They spend all morning and afternoon together.

"Sam is still in the service, he signed up for another tour. Tasha left Hofstra in her senior year and married a doctor. She moved to Baltimore last October. The Beekmans are very upset at her quitting school. They all had a terrible fight and haven't spoken since she left."

Dick goes up to his old room and stares out the back window. Memories of Tasha and a thousand sunsets fade as the gray sky mutes all remaining color. He remembers a line from Eliot: *"There is the empty chapel, only the wind's home."* Deep inside him it is raining. Tomorrow morning he will go back to Jackson Heights.

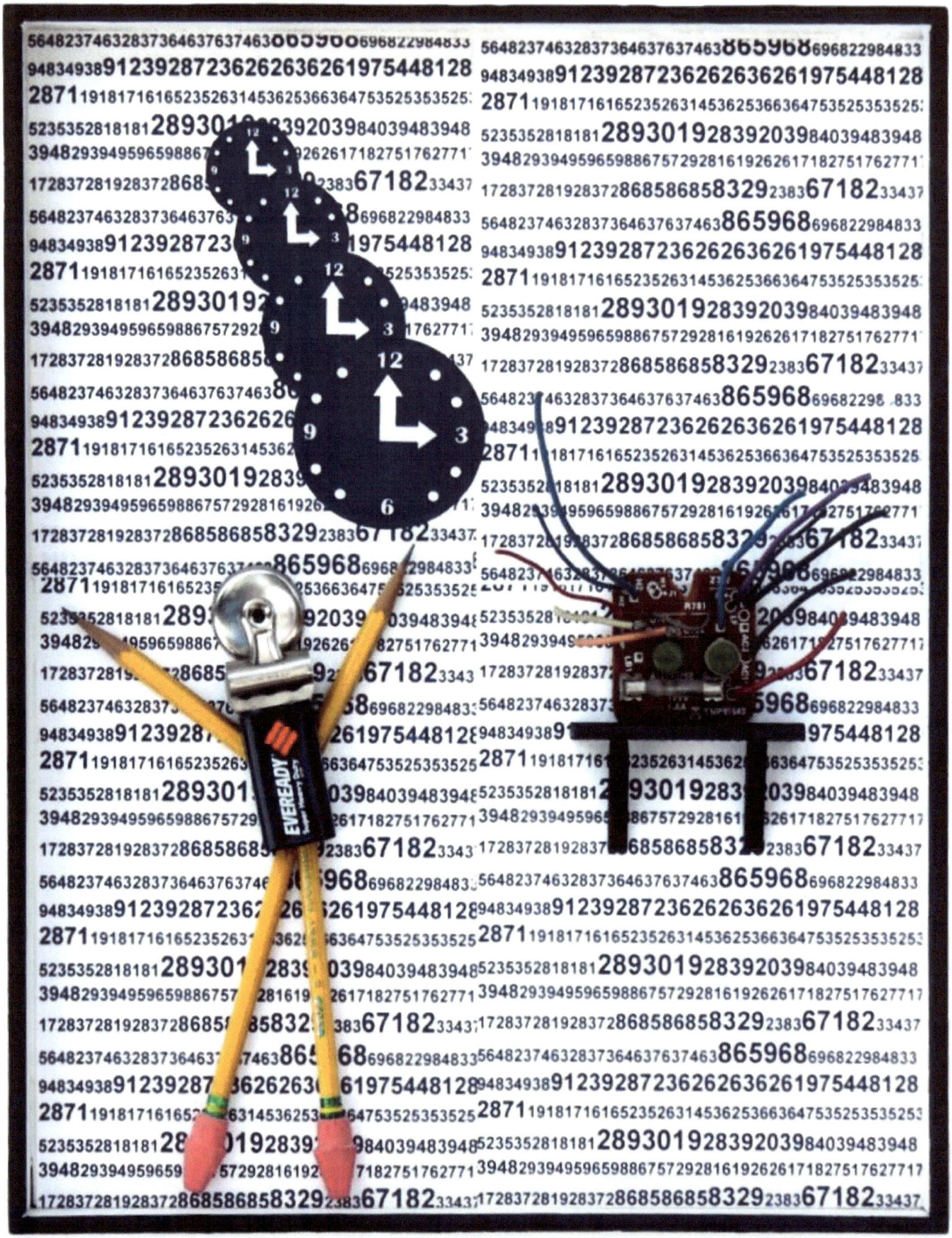
EVEREADY

THE TERRIBLE DAILIES

For the third time in 20 months Dick has changed jobs.
With each change he has more responsibility and makes more money.

This time he lied about having a college degree, and he guessed right:
they didn't check. He is now a junior analyst for Charles Ponzi
Banking & Insurance Corporation.

After two months on the job he is already bored. He remembers an
article in *Mother Nature News* about "The Terrible Dailies," as the
Italians call it. The realization hits him hard. His entire being is
constricted by a routine cycle of have-to-dos without end. Even the
canned music repeats over and over. He is in lockstep.

His boss is a 57-year-old man with a large belly who has worked at
Charles Ponzi for thirty years. The padding on his leather chair has been
squashed flat, and his left elbow has been placed in the same spot
so many times it has worn a groove on his desktop.

"Dicko, you did a great job with this forecast, but you spend too much
time talking to Carol. Now I want you to shape up and pay attention
to business. I need your opinion.
When do you think we should audit our payables?"

Dick usually completes his work in a few hours and starts looking for
a challenge, something new to do, but there is a corporate formula for
everything. He feels totally out of place. He would rather be loading
and unloading trucks like he did last year. At lease he got some exercise.

He takes his lunch to the park. He's not going back to work today.
Maybe he won't go back at all. He rips off a piece of his brown paper
lunch bag and begins to write.

WINDCHIMES
TING WITH VOICES BEADS
OF SHELL AND ~~GLASS~~.
MUMBLE CLUNKS
OF BAMBOO REEDS
WINDOW
HUNG ABOVE THE ~~BOOKCASE~~
SOUND CLICK CLACKS
OF ~~MUSIC~~ TALK.
WE STARE
AT THE BOOKCASE AND

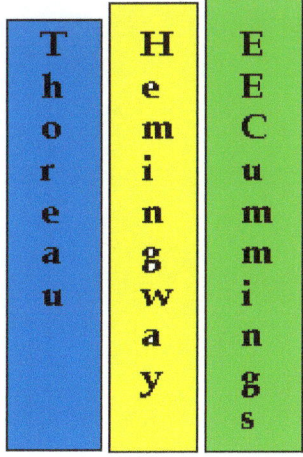

Stare back at us.

They wonder if
as we sing
we remember aged choruses
of vintage words
that have been
written for us.

They see the
darkened silhouettes
of lost cities.

They know the
sound of sand
and the color of music.

We string new
beads of glass and bamboo.

An ancient spirit
enters our song
while our windchimes
chant homage
in awe.

LOOKING FOR LOVE ON BROADWAY

Dick is lonely. He wonders about finding a woman
to share his life with. Tasha is married and living
in Baltimore. He has to forget about her.

Onenightstands have been feeling pretty empty
lately, and besides, who the hell wants the clap?
He wants a companion, a partner, not a social disease.

There is only a round, green velvet pillow next to him
on the eight-foot sofa, and too much space in his closets.

The only voice he hears when he wakes in the morning
is the radio newscaster reporting on the usual atrocities.
By the time he learns that the Celtics edged the Knicks
112 to 110, Dick has finished shaving.

He notices a few white hairs in each sideburn and thinks about
growing a mustache and beard. How would he look? Who cares?

Dick picks up the newspaper left outside his door and flings it
inside the apartment. It lands on a pile of dirty underwear on
the kitchen floor. He will read the paper, do the dishes, and
clean up when he gets home from work.

He turns the key, locking the deadbolt, and accidentally drops his
lunchbox in the hallway. He picks it up and walks to the elevator.

Before he's reached the lobby, Dick has made up his mind. There
are hundreds, no thousands, of attractive women in the city.

All he has to do is find the right one.

BRENDA

Dick, see what I bought, isn't it boofy?
I found it at Bergdorf's.
How do I look?

Let me tell you who I saw yesterday.
I was walking Cuddles and she started yapping
and jumping up and down, and would you believe
it, there was my old roommate, Annie.
No kidding, right there on 7ᵗʰ Avenue.

I haven't seen her in two whole years.
Boy, has she put on weight.

I told her about my new job and guess what?
She's buying a new Chevy from the same dealer
I am! We got different colors. Hers is metallicblue
and mine is kinda orangeypink.

Annie said she has a new boyfriend.
I told her I was seeing you tonight.
Bet her boyfriend's not as cute as mine!

I don't intend to get fat like Annie, so I
just bought a new exercycle at Sears.
I ride it when I get home from work
while I watch TV and eat nachos.
Can you see a difference in my legs?

Gosh, I've been doing all the talking.
Let's talk about you, Dick.

What do *you* think of my new hairdo?

KARLA

Faster! Faster! Can't this car leave some rubber?

Speaking of rubbers, I never make my men use condoms.
There's nothing to worry about. I'm lucky that way.

Want to have some fun? Pull up next to that cop car at
the traffic light. Now put us in reverse and move back slowly.
Did you see the pig stomp on his brakes? The dumb shit
thought he was moving forward. Get a real job, moron!

Look, I got some pills. I don't know what they are, uppers
or downers. My sister pinched them from her doctor's office.
Let's take them and see what happens. Don't worry about
the pig. If he tries to pull us over I'll dump them down a
sewer grate.

Last night I copped a wallet from this guy who was asleep
on my bus. Here's his American Express card. All you got
to do is practice his signature. Let's go to Macy's, they're
open late tonight. We can stock up on some goodies, man.

Wait! Listen, there's a party going on in that building,
upstairs. Look at all the parked cars. Sounds like a live band,
Latino, cool.

No, I don't care that we're in Spanish Harlem, they're having
a good time. I wanna have a good time, too.

Let's go crash it.

TAMMY

Oh Dick, how nice.
You brought me flowers.
My ex-husband never did that.

Jenny likes to eat flowers. She's at that stage
where she stuffs everything in her mouth.
I took Billy and Penny to my mom's,
but Jenny's too active for Mom so
she'll be with us tonight.
Hope you don't mind.

Do you want to hold her? Watch her feet!
Oooops, I'm sorry, she likes to kick backward.
You'd better sit down. Can I get you a glass of water?
Is it very painful?

I'm glad it didn't hurt too much.

Jenny, want to make a peanut butter samitch with mummy
and Dick? She calls it a samitch.
Look at her spread the grape jelly,
she always pours out half the jar.
No, no sweetie, don't pull kitty's tail.

Oooops, I'm sorry Dick.
What a mess.
I'll put your clothes in the washing machine.
They'll be nice and fresh for you tomorrow.

In a couple of hours Jenny will be tired and I'll put her
to bed. We can have a quiet dinner, go to my bedroom
and, you know.

There's no lock on the door
but she probably won't wake up.

SUZAN

Oh Dick, look at the puppy. What a cute little doggie.
Will you buy him for me? Look at his fuzzy tail and
those big fuzzy feet.

Dick, I told you I didn't want to double date with them!
She's a moron and he's a nerd, and I don't want anything
to do with them. They're both just too damn square.

Oh Dick, look at the twins in the baby carriage.
They both have blue eyes and red hair. What are their
names, Miss? Danny and Donny, that's so sweet.

Dick, could you get me some ice cream? Any flavor but
vanilla. Thanks, hon. Shit, why did you get this stuff?
I don't like chocolate either.

Dick, someone's at the door. Oh never mind, I'll get it!
Stop knocking already, give me a chance to get there,
for Chrissake. No I don't want any damn Girl Scout
cookies. Beat it.

What the hell do you mean, you're leaving?
Nobody walks out on me, Dick!
You're just a chickenshit,
afraid of commitment.

I'm throwing *you* out, buddy.
Get out.
Go.

BELLE

You know, Dick, you're the first man I've let in my apartment since Jack and I broke up.

Do you want me to put on some music? I don't have many records, I was always more into science and math.
Now about Neil Diamond?

I'm taking computer programming in grad school. I wrote an accounting protocol that balances your budget and even writes checks. We got a new IBM System 30 I can use whenever I want.

I'm not putting down English or philosophy majors, but I believe in real work, in computers, and in a structured existence. See, I have all my files and equipment lined up by size and color there on my desk. It makes me feel efficient.

Jack used to put paperclips and memo pads in my underwear drawer, just to tick me off. He was always dreaming, looking at the stars, talking about the meaning of life.

It's obvious to me that people created God because they didn't understand how science works. Data and information retrieval, that's the future. The key is to think logically and control your emotions. I'm already investing in technology stocks, and I plan to be a millionaire before I'm thirty. Now all I need is a man who shares my dreams for the future.

You know what really turns me on, Dick?
Come here and look at this. Sexy, huh?
A new keyboard with multi-directional arrows!

SEAL POINT POODLE

It's been two weeks since
Dick moved in with Belle.

They have sex every day
and the sex is very good.

He makes breakfast and dinner.
She does the dishes and housecleaning,
except for the bathroom,
because she has a thing about that.

They both love to read.
Belle likes things neat and tidy
and Dick is trying not to be a slob.

She tries to tell him about computers
and he listens politely.
He tries to tell her about essay writing
and she listens politely.

They have sex every day
and the sex is very good.

Dick pretends to like Neil Diamond at soft volume.
Belle pretends to like e e cummings read aloud.

They discuss buying a pet.
She says she likes the seal point Siamese kitten
he has chosen,
and he says he likes the little black and white poodle
she has picked out.

They have sex every day
and the sex is very good.

THE MAN IN THE MOON

They have been quarreling for two days.
Dick tells Belle not to expect him back until morning and goes
to camp out at the west end of Jones Beach to think things over.

It is July 17th, Dick's birthday, and the temperature had risen to
91 degrees during the day. Now he watches the sun set and a crescent
moon rise. Dick is completely alone, lying on top of his sleeping bag.
He listens to the rustling eelgrass on the sand dunes and feels the
spray of the surf tumbling in.

Belle is pregnant.
She says she's not ready to be a mother and wants to have an abortion.
Dick went crazy when she talked about killing their child.
He shouted at Belle and demanded she have the baby.
He promised he'd do all the work to take care of it.

At nightfall, Dick takes off his clothes and sits naked at the ocean's edge,
foam washing around him. Faint moonlight illuminates the whitecaps
and there is a slight sea breeze.

As the vast sky darkens, little pinpoint lights are born,
one by one by one million, and a shooting star streaks by
for an instant before it dies.

Will the baby be a boy or a girl?
Will Belle love it and be happy once it's born?

Dick decides that the Man in the Moon is the great creator,
and he himself a trusted disciple who has been chosen
to turn on another light.

Dick has created a new person.
He has given the gift of life
as it was given to him.

CITYSCAPE

Belle's apartment is on the Upper West Side
and Dick takes the subway downtown to his job
at Charles Ponzi.

The reading lights of the old train go off and on
as worn-out machinery makes intermittent contact with
the third rail. A defective compressor clanks and whistles,
and the metal wheels squeal around every curve.

The hot air inside the tunnel is rank, and
every morning the entire A train express is
crammed full of commuters.
They try to read their newspapers folded neatly
in quarters so they don't overstep their allotted
square foot of space.

Dick is lucky, he's close enough to grab
a white pole for support. Many people are tossed about
as the train stops and starts.
A large woman with a black veil sits in the single seat
next to the engineer's booth and loudly prays her rosary.

Dick leans against the pole, but he is not truly in the subway.
He is leaning against the redwood and wire dune fence
at Jones Beach.
He remembers rolling down the hill with Sam
on the meadow next to his house, both of them
yelling with irrepressible joy.

Concrete breaks down. Steel corrodes.
Homeless people sit next
to Wall Street executives,
and discarded copies of the Daily News,
not fine, white beach sand or spring grass,
is the carpet under Dick's feet.

CHOOSE A OR B

A – John Hammond
B – Bobby Vinton

A – Manicotti
B – Big Mac

A – West End Beach
B – The IRT subway

A – Raise my child where life is sane and simple
B – Raise my child where the air is foul and criminals rule the streets

A – Find a generous and kind woman who believes in magic
B – Try to live with a woman who has a heart the size of a peanut

A – I am the captain of my ship, I am the master of my soul
B – I am the third mate of my fate, I am a soul out of control

A – I am whole and entire, the universe is within me
B – I pray to anyone with power, forgive me, forgive me

A – To thine own self be true
B – At Charles Ponzi I do what I have to do, and I am what I do

A – Albert Schweitzer
B – Richard Nixon

A – Honda Nighthawk
B – Buick station wagon

A – Write my novel
B – Find a reason to put it off

A – I deserve to be happy
B – I must do my duty

FIRST DEATH

The folded flag rests on the coffee table
next to a picture of Sam in uniform,
wearing his medals proudly.

Mr. and Mrs. Beekman,
Tasha, who is eight months pregnant,
and her husband, Dr. Edward Stone,
sit in silence on the long couch.

Friends and family prepare food no one eats.

It has been six years since he has seen Tasha.
Dick's thoughts run together in rapid fire.

*...another few months and the war would have been over...the
Playboy magazine on Willow Rock...how beautiful Tasha looks,
what a jerk to let her get away...Belle in the apartment, also eight
months pregnant...I don't love her...there's Sam's baseball glove...
I don't know what to say or do...*

There are no greetings, no questions, no talk.

Dick throws one arm around Mrs. Beekman
and the other around Tasha.

They all cry the kind of crying that is inconsolable,
that only stops
when there are no more tears left.

SEE DICK RUN AGAIN

At 9 a.m. on Monday, accounting department
personnel are arriving at Charles Ponzi Corporation's
offices on the 15th floor. They chat about the new
French restaurant on Madison Avenue, the
unusually warm weather, and the shows they
saw on TV over the weekend.

Dick's office is empty.
His desk drawers are empty.
The top of his desk is bare
except for the telephone and stapler,
and his resignation letter,
taped at all four corners
to the fake oak veneer.

PART THREE

CITY LIGHTS

Half an hour before sunrise on March 7th, a fourteen-foot
Ryder truck crosses the lower level of the Williamsburg Bridge,
headed out of Manhattan. Its driver is having a little trouble
staying in his narrow lane. City lights from both shores reflect
on the East River, diamond sparkles that will soon fade as day
breaks and makes them invisible.

Dick is leaving New York for good. All his possessions are loaded
in this rented truck, and he's going back to Greenville.
Mendelssohn's Concerto in E Minor is playing on WQXR.
He holds the steering wheel with his left hand.

Sleeping soundly against his right shoulder is his one-year-old
daughter. He has made a cushion out of his jacket and has half
of it covering her legs. The seat belt is wrapped around both of
them, and his right arm tirelessly cradles his tiny companion.

Rush hour has not yet started as he drives north toward the
Tappan Zee Bridge. Dick wonders if happiness can ever exist
without sadness. He is so happy to be driving home with the baby,
but he has left Belle in the apartment, her new one with private
balcony, uniformed doorman, and in-house security.

How could she tell him to go without her?
How could she say that she hates looking after their child?
How could she give him full custody, and calmly announce that
she'll visit once in a while? How could she say all of that, look him
in the eye, and not shed one tear?

The sun is fully up now, and the light awakens Samantha.
Dick pulls into a Pancake House restaurant
and gas station to refuel.

"Okay, little guy, let's go get some pecan waffles with maple syrup."

GRANDMA

"Don't talk like that in front of the baby."

"I know, Mom, I'm sorry,
but Belle *is* a selfish bitch.
This poor kid will always have to live
with the fact that she was rejected.
I have to be her mother and father.

"Why does she throw up this toddler food?
The doctor says she isn't allergic.
I switched to a more expensive powder.
Will this one cure her rash?
Last week she started waking up at 2 a.m., crying.
Do you think something is wrong?

"I know she misses her mother.
The only time she's happy is when I hold her,
but I'll have to work all day at some bullshit job."

"Don't talk like that in front of the baby."

"Thanks for agreeing to take care of her, Mom.
I'm glad you have the summer off,
but what will we do in September, put her in
some rat bastard's daycare warehouse?"

"Don't talk like that in front of the baby!"

HALF MOON

Dick and Samantha sit on Willow Rock, on a
blanket folded three times so it will be softer.
The old tree was cut down and there is
now skyspace to view the stars.

Samantha is 20 months old and sucks her thumb.
It is 9:30 and the baseball field lights have been turned off.
They are alone.
Dicks sings a Janis Joplin song
while he claps Samantha's hands together.
She is cackling with glee.

Half moon, nighttime sky,
Seven storms from seven seas.
Your love brings life to me,
Your love brings life to me.

He prays for a happy life for his daughter.

Little guy, do you know why Mr. Moonman is only half full?
Because his other half is Mrs. Moonman,
and she's on the other side of the universe.
He has been searching for her a babillion years.
Those little stars are angels with flashlights,
and they are helping him find her.
They're looking in the Big Dipper.
Now they're running around Saturn's rings.
Uh oh, they're spinning out of control in the Orion Nebula,
and Pluto is barking at them!

Let's go home, kiddo.
Too many damn mosquitoes.

French Roast

Colombian Supremo

Espresso Roast

Choc. Raspberry Decaf

Nantucket Blend Decaf

COLUMBIAN SUPREMO

I'm glad I rented the old Barcombe house.
Sammie will have that huge yard to play in,
and I've known all the neighbors for years.

Dick sits in the employees' cafeteria
at American United Corporation,
sipping a cup of strong black coffee.

AMUCO seems like a good company to work for.
The people in here *look* happy,
and there are lots of hip coffee flavors.
Dick smiles to himself, wondering what
Nantucket Blend Decaf tastes like.

I can wear casual clothes and they've got flextime,
which is great for single parents.
Plus the salary is almost what I was making in New York,
hard to get around here.
And it's only a ten minute drive from the house.

I wonder how many projects they'll let me work on.
In Human Resources they talked a lot
about variety and challenge.
They do seem receptive to new ideas,
so maybe it will be an interesting job.

I've got a family now, responsibilities, commitments.
I have to overlook the bullshit, all the stuff
that gets on my nerves.
I have to keep focused on the big picture.
I can do it for Sammie.

This company is growing fast.
Everything is changing.
Change is good.

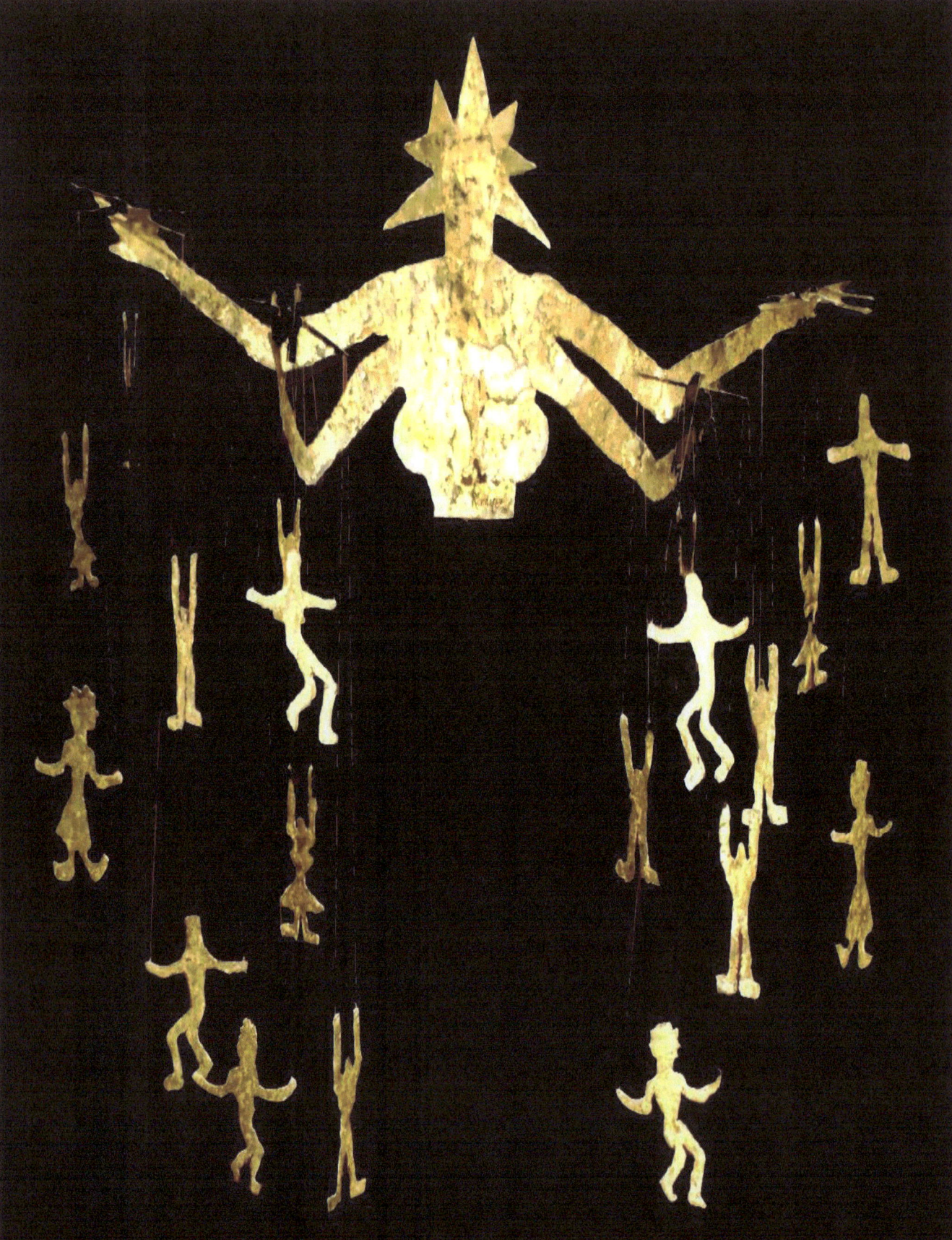

AMERICAN UNITED CORPORATION

Ms. Drummond is showing Dick the recently completed work area in building E. She is five foot eleven, fiftyish, shaped like a Bartlett pear, and wears a charcoal gray business suit. They march together across the freshly polished tile floor, his boss's high heels clacking loudly.

"Dick, this is your new office. It's an environmental prototype we've designed to increase employee output and communications, while trimming costs at the same time. It's called a cubicle.

"Dick, how long have you been at AMUCO? About four months, isn't it, and in my department for two weeks. Are you going to buy a house, get married, and stay in the area? I don't invest time in an employee who doesn't intend to make this his career.

"Dick, I want you to know that we are a progressive company. We were among the first in the state to make recycling mandatory. We don't care what you stick on the inside of your cubicle as long as it isn't obscene or too heavy for the fabric. Everyone on this side of the blue doors must wear a tie, but a jacket is optional.

"Dick, you come highly recommended and I'm told you're a good worker. I've adjusted your salary to pay for additional daycare for Sabrina -- I'm sorry -- for Samantha. When we get into overtime situations, you'll be putting in a lot of extra hours.

"Dick, move in sometime today, will you, and start familiarizing yourself with our systems. Oh, one more thing. They tell me you've got a lot of original ideas on team building, but I'll be frank with you, this is the end of our fiscal year and I want you to concentrate on our data base for the next quarter.

"Dick, your first assignment will be to audit our payables."

A G N I

BOSTON UNIVERSITY ■ CREATIVE WRITING PROGRAM
236 BAY STATE ROAD ■ BOSTON, MASSACHUSETTS 02215

Thank you for letting us consider your work.

THE EDITORS

THE
NEW YORKER
20 WEST 43rd STREET
NEW YORK, N.Y. 10036-7441

We regret that we are unable
to use the enclosed material.

Thank you for giving us the
opportunity to consider it.

We shall not be using your manuscript.
Thank you, however, for giving us the
opportunity to consider it.

Sorry ...

THE BELOIT POETRY JOURNAL
BOX 154. RFD 2. ELLSWORTH, MAINE 04605

Prairie Schooner
P. O. Box 880334, University of Nebraska
Lincoln, NE 68588-0334

We thank you for submitting the enclosed
manuscript for our consideration. We regret that
we are unable to accept it for publication.

Hilda Raz, Editor

▲▲▲▲▲▲▲▲▲▲▲▲▲▲▲▲▲▲▲▲▲▲▲▲▲▲▲▲▲▲▲▲▲▲▲▲

Thank you for sub......
but I'm afraid we can't use it in
The Threepenny Review at present.

HE THREEPE REVIEW

Yale University, Box 208243, New Haven, CT 06520-8243

We want to thank you for your kindness

in letting us see your work, and we regret

we must use this form to let you know

it we have not found a place for it in

The YALE REVIEW

The AMERICAN POETRY REVIEW

1721 Walnut Street • Philadelphia, PA 19103

Thank you for giving us the opportunity to read your manuscript. After much consideration, we feel unable to use the
enclosed material for publication. We regret that the large
volume of submissions precludes a more personal reply.

THE EDITORS

carefully ▪
cannot keep the wo...

Although we would like to senu ▪
response to everyone, and particularly to ▪
who request comment or criticism, the large
number of submissions we receive and the small
size of our staff prevent such correspondence.

We appreciate your kindness in offering this
work and your interest in *Poetry*

THE EDITORS

---

ew England Review
MIDDLEBURY COLLEGE, MIDDLEBURY, VT 05753
802-388-3711 Ext. 5075

We're unable to use this work,
but thank you for your interest.

--The Editors

Please note:
Manuscripts are not read between 1 June and 1 September.
Manuscripts *cannot be responded to or returned* unless accompanied
by a stamped, self-addressed envelope.

MR

the MARLBORO REVIEW

Mr. Richard Brown
371 Oak Ridge Road
Greenville, NY 10107

Dear Mr. Brown:

We are happy to inform you that your story,
The Short Happy Life of Desmond O'Grady, has
been accepted for publication and will appear
in our Fall issue. I really liked the picture you
drew of the main character, and the ending was
a total surprise and delight. We are also
holding your poem, *Windchimes*, for
publication in a future issue.

Please send us a short, 75-word bio and feel
free to submit other material. We look forward
to seeing more of your work.

You will receive a twenty-five dollar
honorarium as well as six author's copies of the
issue containing your story.

Best Wishes,

the Marlboro Review, Inc.
P.O. Box 243, Marlboro, Vermont 05344

JACK DANIEL'S WHISKEY

"Richard Brown, it's been a long while since I saw you last. You look
a lot better now than you did on that occasion. Dear God, that band
was awful. What did you call yourselves, Discombobulators, no,
Argamemnon, that was it. At least you had a creative name, heh heh.
What are you up to now?"

"I work at AMUCO, where else? How about you, Father Doyle?"

"Me? I've been retired for three years. I play golf, pray, and I come
here to McBell's every Thursday night to drink too much Jack Daniel's.
I didn't know it was your favorite whiskey as well. You didn't learn
that from me, you rascal. Why are you in here alone? What do you
do up at AMUCO? Do you like your job?"

"No. I'm in prison, Father. I can touch both sides of my cubicle.
I despise it, but I can't quit because I have a daughter to take care of."

"Little Samantha. I met your mom and daughter in the market last
week, what a beautiful wee lass. She should be baptized, you know.
Richard, you aren't doing her any favors by sacrificing yourself.
You'll wind up a bitter, sick, gray old man before you're forty, and
you'll hate her for it. You used to write so well, why did you stop?"

"I haven't stopped. I just got a story accepted by the Marlboro Review."

"You don't say! The Marlboro Review in Vermont? You don't say. See,
I knew you could do it. Why don't you get a job on the paper? The
Daily Clarion needs you. Their reporters aren't very good."

"Won't work. I don't have a journalism degree."

"So, start your own paper like you did in high school. Why not?
The Clarion could use some competition. Start small with a
four-page weekly. All you need to learn is how to sell ads."

"Sure, Father. And where do I get the money?"

THAT WHICH IS WITHOUT

There must be something.

Good God, there must be something I can do for a living
that I don't utterly hate.
It's not like I haven't tried to find it.

I've been searching for the right work.
I've been searching for the right woman.
I've been searching for every goddamned thing.
When do I get to stop?

I feel like some dumb-ass shark that has to keep swimming
or sink to the bottom.
Bad fluid dynamics, Mr. Shark.
Bad corporate fit, Mr. Brown.

I'm a writer. That's what I am.
I'm a writer, so that's what I have to do.

A treadmill never stops moving. You have to step off it.
But how, and when, and what next?

Right now?
Right now I have to total two months' worth of production output.
We're 30 days behind in sending out invoices, and the internal audit
is behind schedule. It's all been dropped in my lap.
It would be more interesting to count pencils.

When Sammie is in kindergarten, and the teacher asks her
what her daddy does, I don't want her to say,
"He's some kind of clerk at AMUCO."

"He's a writer," she'll answer proudly. "He's a writer!"

But how, and when, and what next?
And how long do I have to hang on?

WOMEN
WHO
LOVE
TOO
MUCH

SECOND DEATH

"You must be Grace, Dick's aunt. I'm Father Doyle.
So sorry about your brother, dear."

"He's buried in Koropi, near Athens. The police say it
was a suicide, but there was no note.
Evelyn was afraid something like this would happen, Father.
She's very upset but not surprised.
I loved Thomas, but he lived an unquiet life and
did not have a strong character."

"How is Dick handling it, Grace?"

"Badly. Outside he's indifferent and he's treating this memorial
service with contempt, but he is clearly suffering inside."

"That family never had a chance to make their peace. Mother and
father on opposite sides of the Atlantic, each with unhealed wounds,
Dick in the middle. Evelyn loved Tom too much, it wasn't good
for anyone..."

"Listen Father, it's Dick's turn to speak."

"I know this will hurt my mother, but I didn't like my father. I
didn't like the way he treated us, and the way he ran off and left
us. But he did teach me one thing worth knowing. He taught me
not to be like him. I want everyone in this room to understand that
we all leave a legacy behind for the next generation. My daughter
has a father who loves her, and accepts her for who she is, and will
never leave her. My father always made it clear that I wasn't
enough, that what I did wasn't enough.

"Except once, for two summer days at the end of a wooden fishing
pier at Zach's Bay on Long Island."

THAT WHICH IS WITHIN

"Hello Grace, this is Father Doyle. How are things on Long Island? I'm calling because I want your opinion on a financial matter. As you know, after the memorial service Dick decided to start a weekly newspaper and last week applied for a loan at Greenville Federal."

"Yes, I know, Father, but they turned him down. He wants to go ahead anyway, but I don't see how he can manage it, even if Evelyn helps with Samantha. I thought it was such a good proposal. I can't imagine why they refused the loan."

"Because one of the bank's trustees, James J. McSuee, is also publisher of The Daily Clarion, that's why! No doubt he fears some honest competition. Dick can't crack that good-old-boy power structure, but I have an idea how to do an end run around it. I have a bit of money saved and can loan Dick $5,000. Grace, can you match that figure?"

"Yes, I can."

"Splendid! It's not much money, but I know our man and he'll make a go of it."

"I suppose he can convert the spare bedroom in that rented house to an office, Father. Oh, I do think it could work. I can't wait to tell Dick."

"I think every free spirit needs a mentor to show him how to fly. When Dick was a teenager he got thrown out of the nest and crash-landed, so to speak. Nobody was there for him. We must be there for him now. In the Gonostic Gospels, which believe me I didn't learn about in the seminary, St Thomas tells us that Christ said, 'If you bring forth that which is within you, that which is within will save you. If you do not bring forth that which is within you, that which is within will destroy you.'

"Dick must start his newspaper."

THE OTHER PAPER

mifbkieglof

"No, no, Sammie, don't touch the typesetter.
Wait, I'm going to save this. You just typed
your first word you little monkey, *mifbkieglof.*
How would you like your own column? I'm
afraid you're too avant garde, you must
remember who our readership is.

"What readership? I have no stories, no photographs,
no ads. I don't even have a name for our paper.
Where do we start? I must be crazy. All I have is
this old printer's box full of abstractions.

"How am I going to support us on dreams? I know
Father Doyle and Aunt Grace believe this will work,
but I'm not so sure. Maybe I should give the money back.

"No. Little guy, we're going to do this. We're going to
turn these dreams into real words on real paper.
We *will* have a weekly, and I'm never going to shovel AMUCO
shit ever, ever again. (I know, I know, Mom. Don't talk
like that in front of the baby.)

"There's going to be another paper in Greenville.
We are the other paper.
Wait! That's it, Sammie! That's our name.
The Other Paper."

DICK AND GOLIATH

"Good morning, my name is Richard Brown, and I noticed your ad in the Clarion. I'm offering one month's free advertising in my new weekly. I'll run the same ad and it will be mailed to every household in the county. A stack of papers will be dropped off at every convenience store and gas station. They are free; you'll get great exposure. No, of course we don't have as many readers as the Clarion, not yet."

"Hi, my name is Richard Brown, and I saw on TV how you and your neighbors are refusing to pay property taxes. The City Manager is starting legal action against you, and I'd like to get your side of the story for my paper. No, I'm not with the Clarion, I'm editor and publisher of The Other Paper, Greenville's new weekly. Naturally you haven't heard of it, ma'am, I just said we're new."

"Why won't you distribute the paper? Aren't you an independent? Never mind about credit, I'll prepay every week. Oh, I get it. McSuee's check is larger than mine. Forget it, who the hell needs you? I'll do it myself."

"What do you mean there's a paper shortage? That's bullshit! I've got a substantial print run here, 20,000 to start, that's good business for you. Okay, buddy, I'll get a printer elsewhere."

"You are who? The zoning commissioner? What zoning violation?
What the hell do you mean I can't have a home office?
This isn't retail!
It isn't a permitted use and you won't grant a variance, eh?
I wonder how you learned about my office.
Up yours.
You tell McSuee this paper will be published if I have to
set up a printing press in *his* bedroom."

MATCHMAKER

"I know your first issue comes out in a week, but you've got to take some time off. Friday is your birthday. You always go camping on your birthday. Why don't you go camping?
Dick, I met a really nice girl I know you'll like. She's attractive, intelligent, and has such a sweet disposition. Her name is Becky Lindel, she comes from a fine family, and she loves to read. Why don't you ask her to go camping with you and Samantha?"

"Give it a rest, Mom."

"You can't spend 16 hours a day, seven days a week, putting together a newspaper! Don't you want companionship? You're going to turn into an old recluse with a wrinkled brow and holes in his socks. You're going to be known as the town frowner. Here comes Dick Brown, with the frown of renown."

"Ha ha! Give it a rest, Mom."

"What are you going to do if some sexy young woman wants to get to know you? I know, you'll invite her to help you glue down ads with rubber cement. Wait, for a really fun time, you can proofread and alphabetize your new subscribers' list!"

"I can tell you're just warming up, Mom.
You're in rare form today."

"My son the stalwart boulder, the serious boulder with moss growing on his north shoulder and toadstools all over his head. My son the boulder, growing older..."

"Okay, okay, I'll call her just to shut you up."

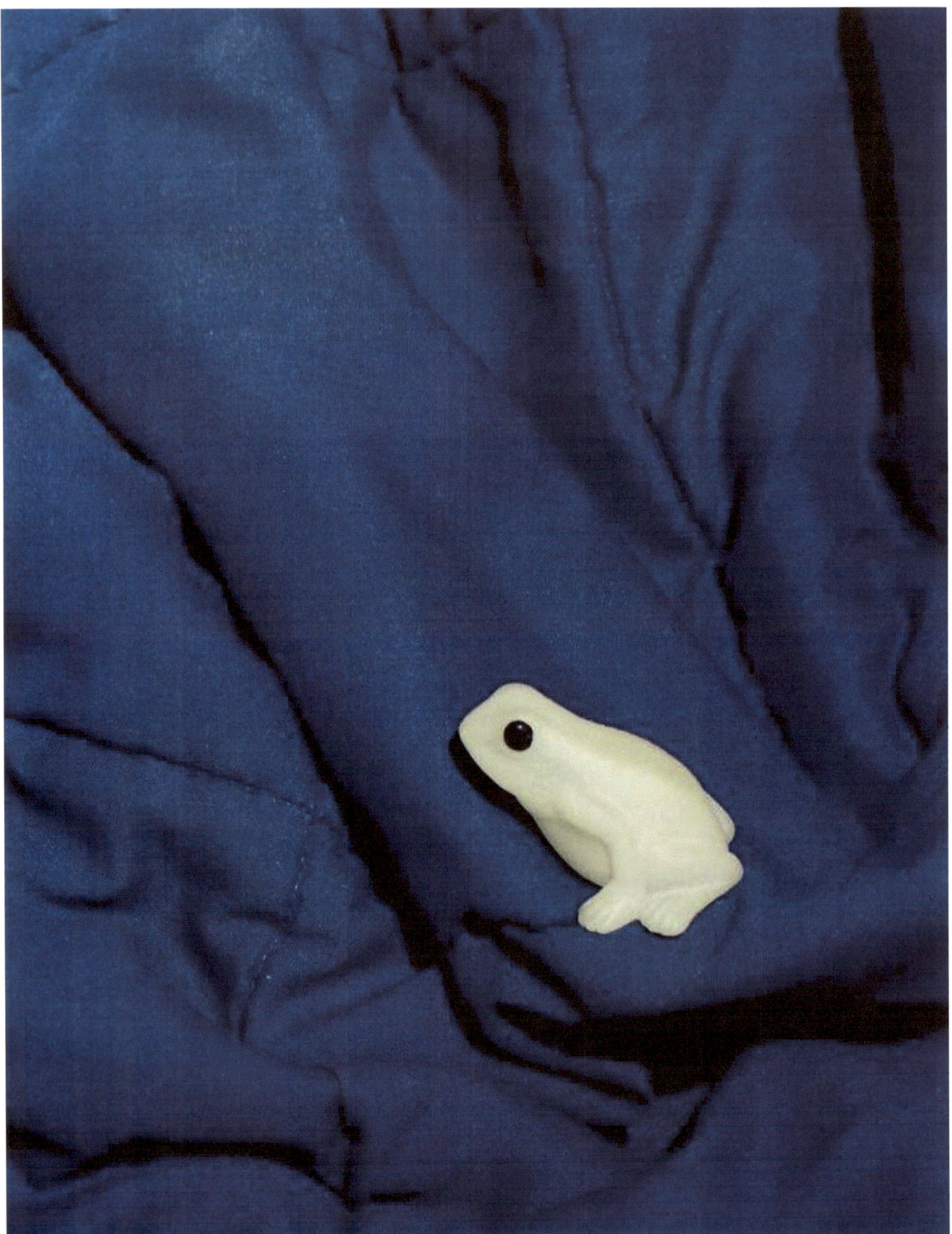

FREDDIE

"What's that?"
"It's a Great Horned Owl. Usually they wait until it's very dark before they start hooting. I can't remember hearing one this early."

"I didn't know owls had horns. What's that thumping sound?"

"Oh, that sound. Becky, that is the sound of the Great Marshmallow-Stealing Quahog. He doesn't have any legs so he uses his squishy body to catapult himself from place to place. Seriously, don't worry about the forest, there's nothing in these woods that will hurt you. I remember when I was a boy on my first overnight camping trip, my father scared the shit out of me by hiding in the woods outside my tent, breathing heavily. I thought he was some primeval lizard. The little black flies and mosquitoes are the only real threat, and they're just a nuisance."

"Dick, I'll put my sleeping bag next to the door, in case I want to go outside in the middle of the night. Sammie can sleep right between us. Okay, I'm going to change into my jammies, no peeking. Oh, look at Sam's little sleeping bag. Isn't that cute? Are you sure you should let her play outside the tent? What are all those lights?"

"Fireflies. Will you relax? I thought you liked to go camping."

"I think I do. Actually, I'm not sure. Well, time to crawl into the sack, night Dick, night Sammie. What's this? Oh my God! Oh my God! Oh my God! Give me the car keys, I'm getting out of here! I'll pick you both up tomorrow."

"Daddy?"

"Yes, Sammie?"

"I don't think Becky liked Freddie. I put him in her sleeping bag. I wanted it to be a surprise. I thought she could play with him. Did I do bad?"

"No, er, yes, er, I don't know. Ha ha, let's bring Freddie back and give him to Grandma."

CISSY

"Well, this is where we live, and this is Sammie. Sammie, say hello to Jill. This is my mom. Mom, this is Jill Crawford, she's a fitness instructor at Gold's Health Club. Thanks for watching Sammie today, Mom, see you tomorrow. Sammie, why don't you show Jill the picture you made. I'll go and order us some pizzas. Jill, what do you want on yours? An extra-large plain cheese sounds great to me, too. I'll get a small anchovy and garlic for Sam. She loves anchovies.

"Sammie, Jill and I have been dating for about two weeks and she wanted to meet you, so be nice and make her feel welcome.

"Sammie! You spilled paint all over her dress. Jill, I'm sorry, she should have been more careful. It's just watercolor, so I hope it washes out okay. Sammie, say you're sorry. Cissy did not do it, you did. I know it was an accident, but now Jill has a big purple splotch on her tummy. How would you like it if someone spilled purple paint all over Cissy? That's her favorite teddy bear, Jill.

"Am I going to be a famous newspaper publisher? Jill, that's an interesting question. Right now I am about 30 days away from losing my storefront lease and my first issue has already been delayed three weeks. I've got my Aunt Grace and Father Doyle volunteering to help launch it, but they only work part-time. My competition is a mega-media giant who employs 375 people. So far the idea of fame hadn't occurred to me. Is that important to you?

"Oh good, the pizzas are here. No, Sammie, you can't have any wine, not for another twelve years, so get used to your grape juice.

"Sammie! What do you mean you wanted to share your anchovies? You made Jill sick! You put an anchovy in her food when we weren't looking. What do you mean it was an accident? You put it in her ice cream and put chocolate sauce on it! Cissy did not do it, you did.

"Jill! Jill! I'm sorry. No, wait!"

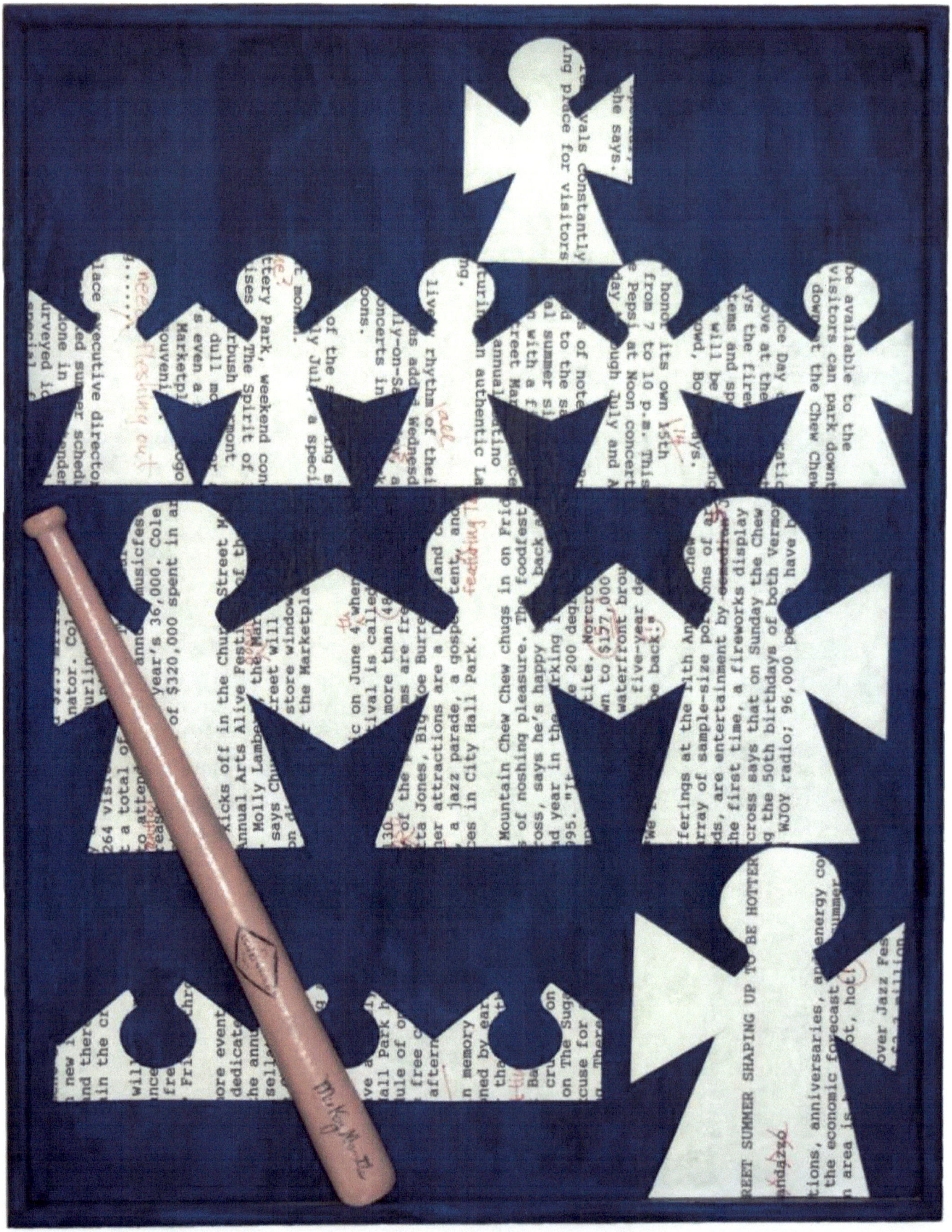

LITTLE ANGEL

"Sammie, this is Liz, our new reporter. Remember now, you're included in our date because you promised to be good. Liz, please pass the fried rice. I got us chicken lo mein, beef and bean sprouts, and lots of egg rolls. Sammie loves them with hot mustard sauce, don't you, Sam?"

"No."

"Where is Sam's mother?"

"In Germany. She's the CEO of Global Oil Company. We haven't heard from her in almost five years, and as far as I'm concerned she doesn't exist. It's been hard on Sammie. She needs a role model."

"What happened to that back window?"

"I was teaching Sam how to hit and she smacked the softball, hit a line drive right over my head. I'll fix it tomorrow."

"Wow, that is one strong kid!"

"Sammie, tell Liz about the kitten we're going to get tomorrow."

"No"

"Okay, then you can go to your room and play. Liz, I made some small changes to the article you wrote for the page two spread."

"Changes? My work never needs editing! I take great pains to make my copy perfect, that's why I went to journalism school. I will not do freelance writing for anyone who hacks up my stories!"

"I'm sorry you feel that way, Liz. This is no big deal, just a few minor changes I think will improve the story. This *is* my paper, you know. Let me get your article and I'll show you what I've done.

"SAMMIE! YOU GET OVER HERE THIS INSTANT!"

SNOW IS SNOW, A TREE GROWS, GOD IS GOD

The small child sees
And wonders -

    What is snow?
            and
    How does a tree grow?
            and
    Who is God?

These lovely mysteries pursue him
Until as a young man he replies
With educated confidence -

    Snow is
        that meteorological phenomenon
        formed by the condensation and
        freezing of water vapor.

    A tree grows
        by the process of photosynthesis,
        assimilation and absorption.

    God is
        a creation of man as a reaction to
        fear and a need for the belief in the
        eventual triumph of Good over Evil.

But he grows dissatisfied
Because these answers are not answers
And he comes wiser to ask again -

    What is snow?
            and
    How does a tree grow?
            and
    Who is God?

                by Rita Wedemeyer

WEEKLY, NOT WEAKLY

"Father, did you hear that Sammie cut up Liz's article? Liz didn't have a backup copy and demanded to be paid for it. Dick gave her a hundred dollars. Sammie refused to apologize because she said that Liz is stupid."

"I read it, Grace, and it was awful. Writing as stiff as a lamppost. Dick doesn't have time to do another article before Friday's deadline, but he did come up with a splendid idea. Actually it was Evelyn's idea. She gave him some stories and poems that her students wrote and he's going to use one to fill the space on page four. He wants to have poetry and short essays in every issue and is going to sponsor a writing and photography contest on a different theme each week."

"Is that a good idea for a newspaper? If people think we're too arty or weird they won't advertise."

"Phooey on them! I agree with Dick. There are lots of people who would like to see bloody photos and pornography, and we would sell a lot of papers, but that doesn't mean we should print trash. We have to offer what the Clarion doesn't, good writing and unique features. The poem he chose is marvelous."

"I'm worried about Dick. He's turning into a workaholic without any social life. Sammie keeps chasing away the girls he brings home."

"She's right as far as I'm concerned. They're all a bunch of floozies with selfish agendas. He's better off by himself and celibate."

"Father, you can't be serious."

"He has a higher calling. A relationship would just be a distraction."

"A higher calling? There is no higher calling than a loving relationship. Or would you rather he keep company with a bottle of whiskey and a book of essays by George Santayana?"

"Hmm…maybe bourbon, the Good Book, *and* a woman would be okay."

GOLIATH 1, DICK 0

"Finally, our first issue has hit the streets. It took us three hours to distribute all the store copies. Our mailing went directly from the printer yesterday. By tomorrow or the next day everyone in the county will have The Other Paper. Let's drive to the gas station and see if anyone is picking them up.

"Father Doyle, where are the papers we dropped off? Were they all taken in three hours? Let's go check some other stores.

"I can't find a single copy in the supermarket or the pizza house either. What the hell is going on?

"Let's check out Main Street, there are seven businesses that agreed to carry our paper.

"Wait, look across the street in the restaurant. Did you see what that rat bastard did? He took all the bundles of our papers and threw them in his truck. That's the Clarion's delivery truck! McSuee sent his goons to steal our papers from the drop-off points! He can't be serious. If we saw this in a B movie, we'd never believe it.

"Father, you call the police from the restaurant and give them the truck's license number. Here, I've written it down. Then call Aunt Grace for a ride back to the office. I'm going after him."

GOLIATH STRIKES OUT

"Officer Perez, tell this shithead to open his truck. He's got the back end filled with our papers. I want his sorry ass thrown in jail. Try to steal my papers again, you piece of garbage, I'll break your face.

"Okay, officer, I'll back off, but you ask him who put him up to this. I want those papers back. I can't have them because they're evidence? Oh great, 2,000 copies lost.

"What the hell do you mean you aren't taking him in for questioning? What more do you need? You're saying the papers are free so there's no theft? But he's interfering with my right to do legitimate business!

"Well, what do you know, the TV crew is here. Smile, fartface, you're going to be on the evening news. Officer Perez, how about telling this nice reporter why you aren't arresting fartface. That's more like it, I knew you would do the right thing. See you downtown.

"I know, I know, Aunt Grace, I took a chance chasing him down. What else was I supposed to do? When I was following that truck at 70 miles an hour, I saw everything we worked for disappearing down the highway. Funny how that TV crew showed up at just the right moment. We got more publicity out of this incident than two years' worth of billboards and promotions would have brought. The Clarion won't dare interfere with us now. The phone is ringing off the hook. Everyone wants a copy of The Other Paper. We'll have to make it bigger or turn away advertisers.

"I wonder who called the TV station?

"Aunt Grace???"

VOLUME ONE, NUMBER 2

"Wait until you read my editorial. I call it 'The Great Paper Chase.' If that driver implicates his boss, probably the circulation director, then perhaps the boss will finger McSuee. It's worth a try.

"Guess what the number one story is, in terms of calls coming into this office? I'm not including curiosity-seekers who saw us on TV, or people who want to subscribe. The piece more people are commenting on than any other is Rita's poem. They want more poems and stories. One reader suggested that we have a literary newspaper, combining local news, photography, and creative writing. We could have subscribers from all over the country. Not a bad idea, but who has time to read all the submissions?

"We need to go to 12 pages right away, and we could easily fill up 16. But it took us three weeks to get out the first issue, and now we have to get the next one out in a week. I never thought success would be such a pain."

Dick, Father Doyle, Aunt Grace, Evelyn Brown, and Samantha finish up their evening meal of pizza, Coke, nachos, cheeseburgers, milkshakes, and pepperoni calzones. It is late and everyone is tired except for Samantha, who chatters about everything to anyone who will listen. Main Street is quiet and the phone has long ago stopped ringing in The Other Paper office.

Appearing suddenly in the doorway are a tall, slender woman and a small child about Samantha's age. They are finely dressed and both have auburn hair. The woman's face is hidden in the shadow cast by the brim of her feathered hat. She speaks in a low voice.

"Hello, Dick. Need any help with the paper?"

TASHA

"We weren't good for each other, Edward and I. He cared much more about his career than he did his family. I tried to be supportive of his goals, too much so in fact, but he didn't meet me halfway. When I learned he was unfaithful it was the last straw. We were separated for over a year, and the divorce was finalized two months ago. I left Baltimore last Friday.

"I've been in touch with your mom for a week, Dick. Don't be mad at her for not telling you; I begged her not to. She told me you aren't involved with anyone. To tell you the truth, that's what decided me to come home.

"I thought about calling you a hundred times over the years, but I was so angry at you! I know you did the best you could, but I didn't deserve to be discarded like that, not after what we had together. Didn't you ever think of me? You could have asked my mother for my phone number.

"That's true, Dick. We couldn't have made things work back then. Our paths were set in opposite directions, and I wound up married and living in Baltimore while you were in New York. You're probably right. How could we reach out to each other when we didn't yet own ourselves?

"You have no idea how much you've changed. You're the same idealistic person inside, but now it shows all over your face. You're not hiding anymore, Dick. I've changed, too, I hope for the better. I used to blame you and my parents for my own problems, and that wasn't fair. They are still upset with me for quitting school and they never did like Edward, but we made peace when Sammy was born. She and I are staying with them until I decide what to do next. I feel both strong and helpless at the same time, isn't that strange?

"By the way, I wasn't a second-rate basketball player, you know. I led the team in scoring my sophomore year. I can be pretty tough. Why am I saying all this? I guess I don't want you to think I have no place else to go. I'm here because.....Oh, I don't know, perhaps I'm kidding myself. They say you can never go back.

"Let's go to McBell's and have a few drinks."

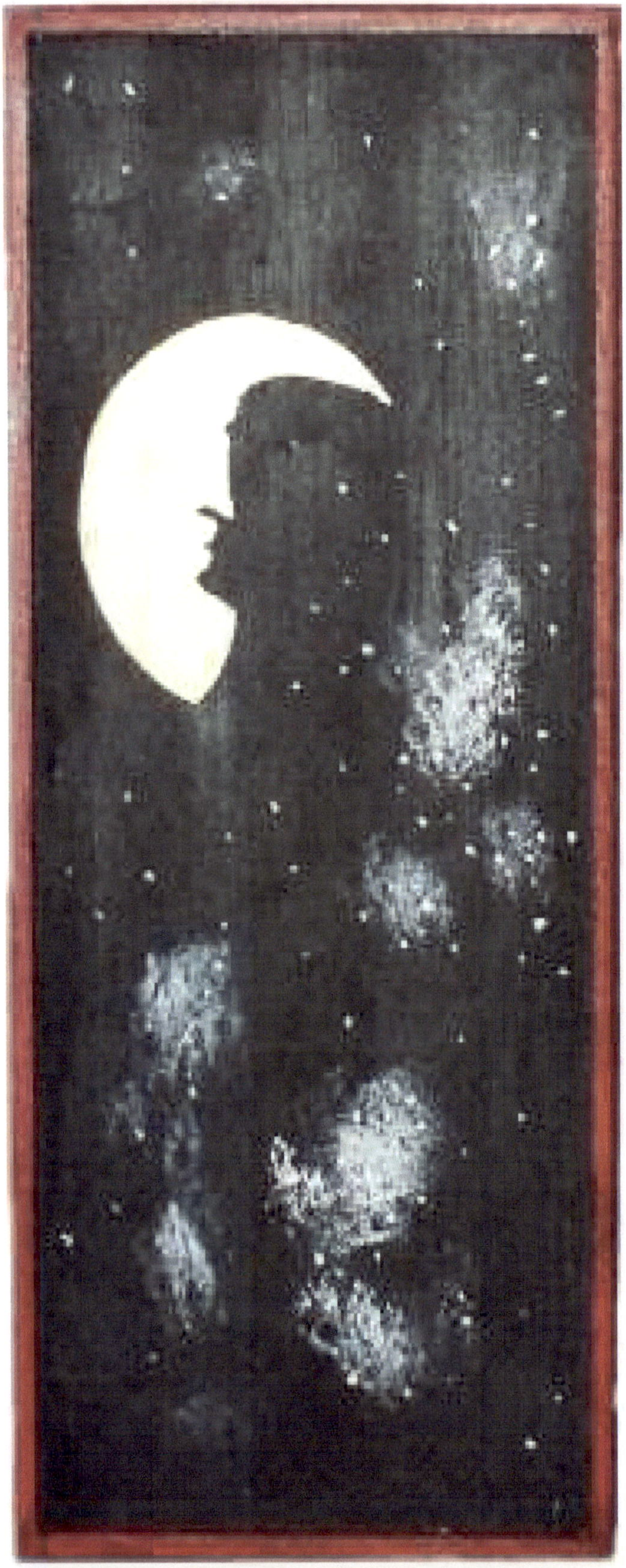

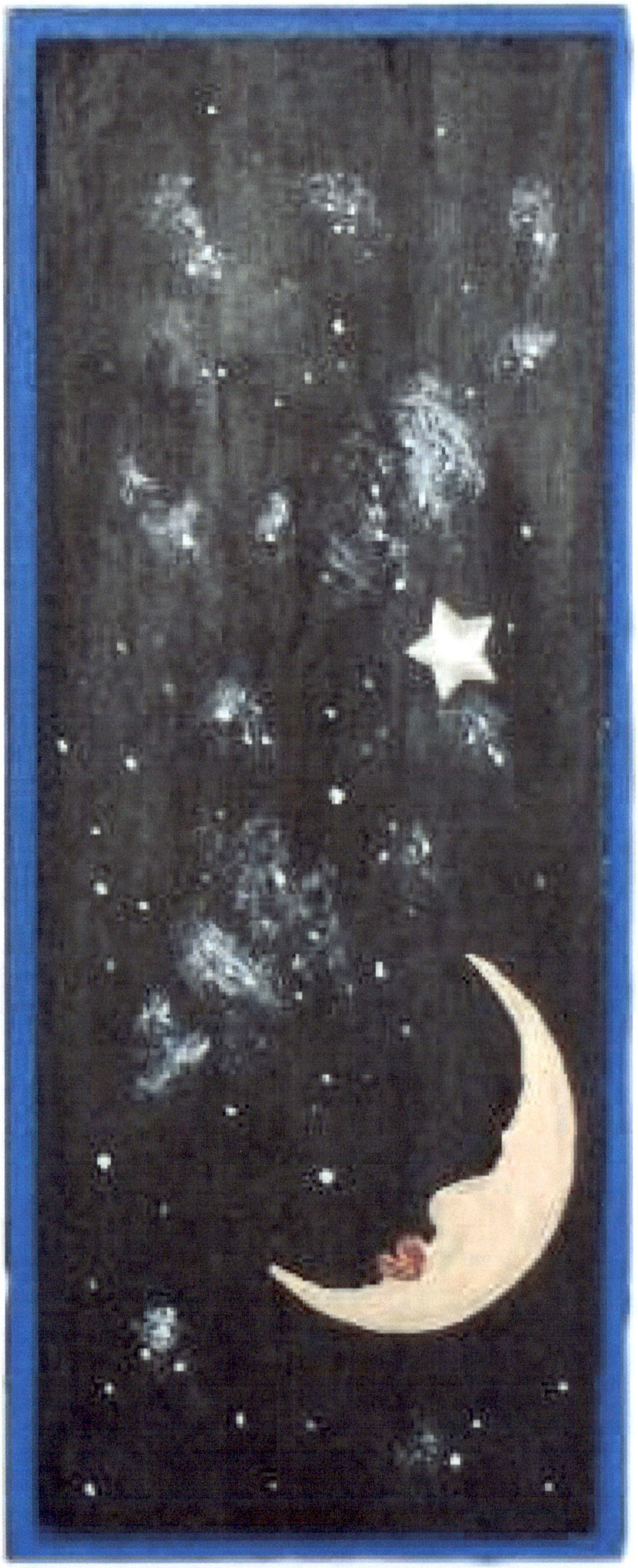

DICK AND TASHA

"Dick, I'm glad you came to the house for dinner yesterday.
My parents love you almost as much as…"

"As what?"

"What do you think of my Samantha? This could get complicated, you
know, two children with the same name. I'm so touched that you would
name your daughter after my brother. I supposed I'm rushing things a
bit but would you like to get together on Saturday? Evelyn agreed to
take care of both kids."

"As what, Tasha?"

"Do you know what your Sammie said to me last night? She said
I was Mrs. Moonman. Who is Mrs. Moonman?

"She's a lovely child, but very different from my Sammy. My Sammy is
reserved, shy and quiet, maybe because Edward and I didn't always get
along. Your Sam is more like me when I was little."

"She's a holy terror who is going to corrupt your Sammy. Then there
will be two monsters. Hey, they can start a kiddy Mafia!"

"A holy terror? You shouldn't talk like that about your own daughter.
She's adorable, and much smarter than you are. You're just jealous
because she likes me."

"No, Tasha, I'm glad she likes you. I don't know what the future will
bring, but I don't want to go there without you. Wherever I go,
whatever I do, I want to come home to you and our two Sams."

"Dick, do you mean that? Me and you, after all this time?"

"I won't answer your question until you answer mine.
As what, Tasha?"

SAMMY AND SAMMIE

"My mom likes your dad. I think we are going to spend a lot of time with our grandmas."

"My dad really likes your mom. We will all live together before long, or I will cause big trouble."

"My dad is a doctor. He ran away because he wanted a new life. Did your mom do the same thing?"

"I don't remember my mom. My dad says she is a selfish bitch."

"What is a bitch?"

"Someone who leaves you because they are stupid."

"Then my dad is a selfish bitch. Do you want to be sisters? Do you like my mom? I think your dad is very nice but he is shorter than Mom."

"My dad isn't short, your mom is too tall."

"She is not!"

"She is too."

"Is not."

"Is too. But she's very pretty. I saw a picture of my mom and she's also very pretty. But I don't care about her. Father Doyle says it's a sin to say bad things about your mother, but I know what I know, and it's a very big sin to run away and leave your family."

"Do you want to go to my grandma's house? She baked some pecan chocolate chip cookies and she will let us watch grownup movies on TV."

"I wonder what Mom and Dad are doing now?"

LAST LOVE

There will never be another.
Her breath like peaches
in my mouth.

There will never be another.
Like the air that lifts a swallow,
like the sea that cradles angelfish.

There will never be another.
Rolling forever down
a meadow of silk and lace.

There will never be another.
He has opened
They are risen.

~the end~

Joe Randazzo has traveled extensively and writes about what he sees. He believes in the heroism of the ordinary working person, the transformative power of love, and the rejuvenating effects of a truly fine pizza. He is the author of four previous books. His artwork has been exhibited at many venues throughout New England including Castleton State College, T. W. Wood Art Gallery, and the Helen Day Art Center.

www.ingramcontent.com/pod-product-compliance
Lightning Source LLC
Chambersburg PA
CBHW040821050726
47507CB00019B/88